CUFFED
A Cautionary Tale of Love, Lies & Betrayal

Parker Washington

Acknowledgments

God, above all, thank you!

It's not easy to come across genuine support from genuine people, but I'm grateful for all of those in my life who truly want to see me win. Thank you to everyone who has ever read and loved or read and *hated* anything I've ever written. Thank you to everyone who has contributed to the content of my work, whether good or *bad*.

Thissy, thank YOU! You've supported me, and this craft of mine since I was ten. If it weren't for you, I'd still be sitting on this talent. I love you. Thanks for always gassing me up. You're the realest. Best sister ever!

Yatt, I appreciate how invested you've become in this. It's so exciting when you come to me with ideas for my next book or characters and titles. Thank you for being even more supportive than you already were. Let's see where this takes us.

To my sisters *Beyond the Pen*, same thing different day with us. I appreciate all our late-night brainstorming and group call writing sessions. I'm grateful that God put you all in my

3

life, as we share the same passion for this gift. There's no turning back now. Only up from here.

In the words of Cash and Caine, "Let's eat."

Dedication

It's all for you, son son.

I love you.

ONE

. . .

With her floral chunky heels trotting down the long, carpeted hallway, Ivyana Atkins carried the last large brown box to her new apartment. With a sweaty neck and stiff arms, she nearly ran to the door, which read 336, as her phone threatened to slip from its position between the side of her face and shoulder. She let out an exasperated sigh wishing she could float. But she was still ecstatic that she was finally moving out of her parents' suburban home and into her own place. She was beginning to feel like a real adult. Her enthusiasm dimmed a little as her sister continued to tease her about her choice of "moving attire".

"You're only allowed to look cute while you move when you have a nigga doing the hard work for you, sis. Your lonely ass should've been sweatpants, hair tied, chilling with no make-up on." Her younger sister joked between hysterical laughter.

"Ha, Ha." Ivy laughed sarcastically with an eye roll.

Trinity Atkins was five years younger than Ivy and while they were best friends, it was moments like this that reminded the two sisters of their age difference. Trinity was a nineteen-year-old, carefree college sophomore living at home while Ivyana was twenty-four and *trying* to live her life as an independent adult.

Initially, Ivy had gotten dressed for a meeting with her boss. But the meeting had been delayed. And instead of changing she opted to get moving—wanting to officially be in her apartment once she returned in the evening. She didn't mind being the butt of her sister's jokes because this was a huge step for her. Besides the joke would be on Trinity when Ivy was all settled and reality set in that she would no longer have her sister by her side all the time.

The scent of cherry almond whisked by and invaded Ivy's nostrils as a young woman walked alongside her in the

7

opposite direction. "Your shoes are so cute." The woman said as she flashed a warm smile toward Ivy. The uneasiness she was feeling about moving into the unfamiliar area subsided, a little. She was still quite nervous about living in the area that some deemed to be the hood. *Especially alone.*

"Thank you." She muttered softly, even though the woman had already made her way toward the elevators.

. "Finally," she sighed in relief as she entered her apartment. She was relieved to finally be putting the heavy box of books down. She was also happy. And grateful to finally be at place where she could call the space behind the brown, wooden door her own.

Ivyana was sure that moving out of the single family, four-bedroom home and into her new small, one-bedroom apartment would be like stepping into a new world filled with some interesting people. But from what she had witnessed so far, the people didn't seem to be so bad. She really didn't mind the fact that she didn't have a porch, big backyard, and finished basement. She was just happy to have the cozy living space.

There was just enough room for her and that was all she needed.

As she wrapped up her phone conversation with her younger sister, a smile tugged at the corners of her mouth. She was proud that she was all moved into her very first home. Granted it was just an apartment and wasn't in the best location, but it was *her home* nonetheless. And she couldn't wait to fix everything up to her liking. She had already envisioned what she wanted it to look like. The mint green bathroom décor, the chocolate brown dining set that went beautifully with the mahogany wooden floors, and of course the grey living room set with red accents that made the small space seem modern and chic. But it would all have to wait, because the only thing she had time to do was put each box in their proper location and grab the box of dark and lovely hair dye.

With a new house, new environment and potentially new people in her life, Ivy felt like a small upgrade for herself wouldn't hurt. She was always shy, quiet, and reserved to those

9

that didn't know her well. And in her mind, that didn't necessarily need to change. But stepping into adulthood officially, she wanted to look the part. And what's better to mark a new place in your life than a change in hair color.

Once leaving out, the day had seemed to turn into early evening and the early spring weather had grown cool although the sun had yet to go down. She hated it. Her birthday was only a week before and it was still winter then, but now the March weather had gone from bitter cold, to sunny and warm most days.

A French Montana song blasted from a black BMW in front of her building, causing her to sing along in her head as she trotted down the sidewalk toward her car. There weren't many people lingering, but the loud music and sound of kids gathering around the nearby ice cream truck made her smile. It definitely wasn't something that she was used to, growing up in a quiet semi-gated community. But it was definitely something she didn't mind getting used to.

Ivy parked her silver Toyota Camry on the sidewalk behind the building and made her way inside of the twenty-second district building to meet with Detective Johnathan Gates, her superior.

"Officer Atkins." He greeted as he sat along the edge of his cherry wooden desk. "This wasn't a meeting per say, but more so a good luck to you. It looks like we're all set." He clapped. "Are you likinp.g the new neighborhood?" He wondered, and she smiled nodding respectfully.

Detective Gates wasn't exactly elderly, only in his early forties, but he was obviously her elder. He was very muscular. He was actually pretty handsome too, with his salt and pepper beard, the small curls on his head that he continuously dyed jet black—*like no one could tell*, and frown lines in his forehead he'd developed from years of stress.

"I love it actually. I honestly didn't think it would grow on me so soon." She admitted, and he nodded in approval. It was him who had helped her find that location, knowing that the environment was perfect for their *task*.

Pulling a large manila folder from his desk and opening it up in front of her, Mr. Gates began to remind her of why she **really** moved, *the task*. Inside of the folder were pictures of convicted members of a top drug organization based out of North Philadelphia that moved throughout Pennsylvania, New Jersey and Delaware. Urban *and* rural.

"We've arrested five individuals tied to this organization over the past six months, yet it seems to still be growing rapidly. These hits aren't bothering them at all. And they're getting more and more dangerous by the day. They are suspected of being cold-blooded killers on top of already being drug dealers. There have been quite a few unsolved homicides. And while there are no leads, something in my gut is telling me that it ties back to this group. None of the young men and women in custody are talking so we're on our own. These twin boys who are rumored to be behind this outbreak of drugs in our city are very smart. We have nothing on them except their street names; Cash and Caine. The goal is to find out who has ties to them and how we can get to them, or at least someone closer to them than the low lives we have now. That's where you come in. Now, you're sure you can handle this?"

Detective Gates had run this same story by her since she received word that she was going undercover for this assignment. But after hearing it right then, she actually wasn't too sure. When she initially signed up to be an officer of the law, she knew the risk she would be taking, however, she wasn't expecting to be in such a predicament so soon. She was only two years into the force, but Detective Gates had handpicked her for this case. She played the back well, which made her the perfect person for the job in his mind.

She had been nervous even when he first asked her. But she knew this case could make or break her career. So of course, when presented with the opportunity, she was all for it. Now though, with her being only seconds away from a new life and the case of a lifetime, she was beginning to get anxious.

"I'm ready." She assured even though she could feel doubt and nervousness creeping up her spine.

Johnathan Gates was pleased with her answer. If she were able to successfully aid in getting those thugs off the street it wouldn't only be a good look for her, but for him as well. He handed her keys to a new vehicle and reiterated for the one millionth time that the details of this case were never to be revealed, mentioned or discussed at any time with anyone. Not even family. Especially family.

Ivy smiled and grabbed the keys. "Don't worry, Mr. Gates. I've got this. Maybe once I'm done I can have your job. Or maybe pursue a career in acting." She joked.

TWO

• • •

The calm evening draft eased into the small crack of the window of Caine's black BMW. He and his twin brother, Cash, sat inside waiting for Akira Francis, their friend and business partner. A thick cloud of a marijuana scented smoke escaped through the crack as Caine puffed from a neatly rolled backwood. Cash rolled his window down a bit further, trying not to catch a contact high. Unlike his brother, Cash didn't care for the drug. He rarely ever drank. He considered himself a businessman and didn't like anything altering his state of mind. And although some could function with it, like Caine, he refused to take that chance. He needed to be ready for whatever, whenever— and he took precautions to ensure that he always would be.

Cash turned down the radio blaring the French Montana song a bit and leaned into the middle console getting Caine's attention. "So, the shipment from Ivan is coming tonight and the shipment from Amani is coming tonight now too instead of next week so we need all hands-on deck to make this shit quick and simple," Cash told his brother with slight irritation in his voice. He wasn't expecting to have so much on his plate and two shipments of drugs coming his way at once. Enough drugs to supply **three** states. Caine nodded his head in agreement. Ivan Hernandez was their Colombian connect. Hernandez was responsible for making sure they always received the best and purest cocaine and he always did.

That alone was reason enough for them to be so successful, but with the marijuana they got from Amani Francis, a Jamaican kingpin and Akira's father, they were sitting *higher* than the top. But everyone knows the higher up you are, the more people will want to knock you down so the two brothers did everything in their power to make sure that they were never caught slipping. They didn't just have to worry about the law. They had to watch out for friends becoming enemies, workers getting greedy, niggas getting knocked and becoming informants, possible set ups. It was hard having to

16

constantly be on your toes and watch your back around even the people who you were closest to. But they didn't mind. It came with the lifestyle they chose to live and neither of them were ready to let it all go. Even for peace of mind.

Caine looked at his phone before he put out his blunt and looked down at the seventeen-thousand-dollar yellow gold Rolex that adorned his wrist. "Well let's go get this shit done. I need to make some calls to make sure everybody is where the fuck they need to be when the fuck they need to be there," he said before putting his car in drive.

"We still have to wait for Kira." Cash reminded before his brother could pull off.

"She just texted me. She's going to meet us there."

"Bet." Cash nodded, leaning back against the headrest. "Let's go get this money."

Although Caine and Cash were identical twins, sharing the same rich, dark chocolate skin and almond shaped eyes that seemed to always be in a natural squint—they were polar opposites. Surprisingly though, it's what made them work so well together. They balanced one another out. Neither of the boys were to be fucked with. Caine was the hot head, take no shit twin who acted on impulse. Cash, on the other hand, was the voice of reason. He was the twin who looked at every situation from every angle before reacting. And could put fear in someone without ever raising his voice.

The black X5 pulled into the dark alley in back of "Chinx", a hot spot bar and grille in the neighborhood owned by Cash and Caine and run by their mother, Celeste. Or best known by her nickname, Chink since she too held those same naturally squinted almond shaped eyes. Cash hopped out of his brother's car to walk the few steps to his own car before the commotion startled the both of them. They were aware that everyone would be on their way, but this wasn't commotion of a gathering group of hungry drug dealers. Following the noise to a small corner of the alley behind a dumpster, Cash and Caine noticed Riz with his gun to the middle of someone's forehead. He didn't bother explaining his actions to the twins, *his superiors*, before pulling the trigger.

At twenty-two Risen Ghould had the heart and work ethic of someone twice his age. He was only a few weeks shy of eighteen when he began working for the twins. And while they didn't want to expose him to the life he was now living, he was already on a downward spiral to destruction. He had been tied to quite a few robberies in the city but with him not being of legal age, he never did real time for it. Just back and forth to and from juvenile detention centers. If the police would have known that Riz was a cold-blooded killer as well, they would've charged him as an adult on any of those cases, for sure. But that was something the twins used to their advantage. They took him under their wing because they knew that if anything or anyone needed to be taken care of, Riz was the man for the job. And their job was to always make sure he was smart about what he did.

Risen was a bad ass kid with dope fiend parents. He was your typical *"product of the environment"*. He had the potential to be better though. He was raised by his grandmother who made sure he was loved, ate home cooked meals every night, went to school in clean clothes every day and helped him with his homework every night. That was until she passed when he was twelve. He knew that his Memaw's untimely passing sealed his fate. He just wasn't meant to be one of those guys. He bounced from group home to group home afterwards. And it was like trouble just seemed to follow him, but he grew accustomed to it. His role models would never be doctors and lawyers or even basketball players or rappers. Neither of them could put someone who didn't have their skill or credentials in a positon like theirs. So, he looked to the only type of niggas he was familiar with. *Street niggas.* A street nigga was always willing to put someone on money and that's why they were more respected in Risen's eyes.

Cash and Caine looked at one another before looking back at Risen. Caine smirked while Cash simply shook his head. "Clean this shit up," Caine told him as he walked over the body and into the back of the building. Cash lingered behind though and scratched his neck, slightly perplexed.

"You out here acting your age, huh bro?" His unthreatening casual tone still made Risen straighten himself up. They had become family, brothers even. Still he knew that at the end of the day he worked for them and there was a mutual level of respect for that.

"Nah. What you mean? I-"

"You out here killing the law?" He chuckled, though clearly not amused. "You trying to bring unnecessary heat to us?" Cash questioned with furrowed brows as if he were truly trying to understand.

"Man you know I'm not-" Risen began only to be cut off yet again by Cash.

"This doesn't even have shit to do with us. This is personal. He sent your uncle away and gave him the needle, I get that. That's still the fucking law and that's some shit we don't need. I'm all for proving points and shit, but you do that shit on your own time." He finished before sighing. All the talk he was doing was pointless. What was done was done. "Hurry up and clean this up. And make sure you get rid of this shit."

21

He told him, pointing toward the gun that hung by his side. "Not hide. Get rid of it."

Cash trusted Riz and his decisions because he knew that he never used his gun unless it was necessary. Caine did too. But moments like this reminded them that he was still that reckless young nigga.

By the time Cash entered the building and stood beside his brother, everyone seemed to be where they needed to be. Akira waltzed in, her heels clicking against the hardwood and echoing throughout the large stocking area they were operating out of. "Why do you always have to be here, daddy's girl?" Caine huffed in annoyance before the scent of coconut oil from her hair tickled his nostrils as she made her way to where he stood.

Akira Francis was Amani's only daughter and while her two brothers still resided in Jamaica working with their father, she was sent to the states to look after their other business ventures. She started off as an annoying, silver spoon fed brat, but over the past couple of years, she had become part of the family. Standing at five feet six inches, with long slender legs, a big, curly fro and smooth, medium brown skin, her presence was always known and powerful.

"Because I fucking can." She whispered, inches away from his face before winking.

Akira was the manager at Chinx. She was needed to do all the things that their mother didn't want to be involved in. Like making sure she was the one signing for the shipments that one would *assume* to be boxes of liquor. Celeste was aware of her sons' business choices because of how close their family was. And while she didn't necessarily agree with them, she loved her boys. She would support them through anything. And she'd beat anyone's ass that dared to question her motherhood. It was the North Philly in her.

Caine smirked slightly and watched Akira's ass jiggle behind the denim jeans she wore. She walked away just as his brother was tapping his arm hearing trucks pulling into the loading space. Akira held up her hand for the boys to stay put while she went outside to make sure they were clear. She signed the clipboard with her name and began to grab a few boxes at a time while the others followed suit.

"Aye." Caine called to Akira who stopped in her tracks abruptly. "Put that shit down." He demanded and before she was able to object, Riz had grabbed the boxes from her hands and walked away forcing a fake attitude to spew through Akira.

Cash and Caine stood against the plain white wall and watched their hard work pay off as everyone scurried to get shit done quickly and done right. Caine smirked, and Cash did the same not even having to look his brother's way to know how he was feeling. He was feeling great. Like the motherfucking man and Cash knew because he was feeling the exact same way. *Twintuition*. "Let's eat." Cash chuckled as he slapped hands with his brother.

THREE

. . .

Ivy gave herself a once over in the mirror as she admired how different she looked. She liked the change and couldn't wait to flaunt it. The twenty-six-inch jet-black weave covered the sandy brown hair she had sported her whole life. She was impressed by the needed transformation. As crazy as it sounded it was like she had become a new woman, her own woman. No longer the deacon's daughter, but Ivy. **Officer Atkins.** Finger combing the long tresses, she smiled at herself, her full lips turning into small slits that her whitened teeth poked through. The dark hair went well with her golden skin. Surprisingly, she looked like her mother who was the most beautiful woman Ivy had ever laid eyes on.

Peeling her eyes away from her reflection, she flipped opened the manila folder to look at the same short file once again. She was more than anxious to get a head start on her work, knowing that this was the real deal for her. But she hadn't gotten much information on the organization she was to be investigating. She only had the information that the department had and it made her wonder. If they had so little evidence, why they were trying to tackle this now? But her job was to do what she was told. The only thing she knew was that she was investigating twin brothers who went by the street names Cash and Caine and the name of a neighborhood they either lived in or visited frequently to do business. "Cash and Caine. Cash and Cocaine?" She pieced together. "That's clever." She giggled as she observed the pages fully as if something new would pop out. But they all still told her the same thing, that these two were the main distributors of crack cocaine, heroin, and marijuana heavily throughout the city. In a nut shell, she had nothing.

These guys were smart though and Ivy found herself wondering how the fuck she would be able to outsmart not one, but two of the most untouchable people in the city. They obviously didn't do any of the dirty work themselves and they did a great job with deciding who would work for them because they all seemed completely loyal. Ivy decided that that would have to be the way to go. She'd have to get through the little people to work her way up. "Now I know why these damn cases take so long." She huffed slightly before hearing her phone vibrate against her nightstand pausing the nineties R&B that blared from her small speaker.

"Zimmy Zim!" She greeted her best friend Zimora happily as she walked around her carpet barefoot. Now that she was alone with no entertainment, a phone call from anyone would've signaled the same reaction.

"Okay bitch! Somebody's happy to hear my voice." She chuckled forcing Ivy to roll her eyes.

"You always ruin it. But I'll let it slide because I miss you." Ivy and Zimora had started off as best friends in fourth grade, fell off from sixth to eighth then picked back up in ninth grade like it was nothing. They hardly ever discussed work, since both of their professions called for confidentiality agreements with Zimora being an attorney and Ivy being an officer. Instead, they discussed celebrity "tea" and gossip from the people they had gone to elementary, middle and high school with.

"I miss you more," Zimora assured. "I wish you get off your high horse and let me hook you up with one of Marcus' friends so we can double date like we did in high school." Ivy huffed and pursed her lips together, contemplating whether or not she wanted to hang up on her friend.

It was no secret that Ivy was single and had been for quite some time. Truthfully, if you asked her she'd tell you that she had never been in a real relationship. Only situation ship after situation ship.

"No thanks, I'm good."

"Ivy," Zimora began in her motherly tone as if they weren't the same age. "You're not nineteen anymore. Every guy you deal with won't be afraid of commitment. But you have to give someone a chance." She told her. While Ivy knew she was right, it wasn't something she was trying to hear. If she happened to find a man worth it, fine. But she wasn't planning to go out of her way to find one. Especially when she had more important things to handle.

Ivy had talked to a few guys, but commitment didn't seem like a goal for these new niggas, so her cookie jar had been closed for the past year. It seemed that when it was known that someone hadn't been having sex it was assumed that they needed to be set up. Ivy wasn't down for having sex with just anyone. Her devout Christian parents drilled into her and her sister that spirits transferred through sex and she was fine with waiting until she had found someone she connected with. It was something she was embarrassed to admit in high school, but she'd broadcast in if she needed to now.

"You're right Zim. I'll give someone a chance. Who did you have in-" she questioned, allowing her own thoughts to contradict her words, but was soon cut off by her best friend's noisy background.

Zimora's husband Marcus' venomous voice boomed in the background and Zimora quickly hung up without saying bye as if Ivy was a side nigga or like she wasn't allowed to talk. Zimora could front, but her best friend knew that her marriage wasn't as peachy as she made it out to be. And that was exactly why Ivy was in no rush to be set up, especially with one of Marcus's friends. "Look at God," she mumbled to herself realizing that she was only a few seconds shy of agreeing to being hooked up with one of his friends.

Marcus and Zimora had met in their sophomore year of undergrad and had been together off and on since. Well, until they got married. They had only been married for two years, but Ivy could tell that her friend wasn't happy. She was only hoping that his controlling spirit and bad temper didn't turn violent eventually.

The thought of her best friend's toxic, unhealthy relationship was depressing and her being home alone didn't stop her mind from wandering. She eyed the time on her phone and figured that taking advantage of the night time air would be just what she needed to clear her head. And adapt to her new environment.

Stepping out of the building into the cool spring air Ivy noticed people lingering more than they did in the day. Men began catcalling as soon as her grey Hurrache sneakers hit the pavement and she didn't even grow offended. That, along with the congested stoops and loud music seemed to be the norm. And while her parents considered it to be ghetto and distasteful to be so loud and inconsiderate, she was already enjoying it.

FOUR

. . .

Dakota Summers waltzed into *Kingston's* for some of the city's best Jamaican and Caribbean cuisine, letting her feet lead her through the crowd of people standing around.

"Kira, give me an oxtail platter, rice, and peas, cabbage and throw in some wings. Jerk sauce on the side because you're always trying to kill me with that shit." A tall, medium built dark skinned guy said to the woman behind the counter. He seemed to be a regular there by how he interacted with her, but Koko couldn't recall ever seeing him.

"Whatever." Akira hummed before looking behind him toward Dakota who was next in line, letting her know that all of the other people lingering were simply waiting to be served. "What can I get you, sweetie?"

"Uh, could I have the jerk platter with rice and peas and cabbage. Add plantains too, please and sauce on the side."

"Oh now everybody wants their sauce on the side." The guy before her joked causing her to roll her eyes.

"Boy, don't be in here harassing my customers," Akira warned as she handed a few finished platters to those who were waiting.

Dakota sighed in annoyance when the same guy made his way over to what she had deemed her waiting area. "Don't flatter yourself too much, ma. I'm waiting for my food just like you." He informed in a semi hushed tone, making her feel a little bad about her annoyance toward him. He hadn't necessarily done anything, but it seemed like any nigga that spoke to her had a sense of entitlement. They felt entitled to a conversation, a date or a phone number. All she wanted to do was get her food and lounge around for the night after such a long day.

To her surprise, he didn't say anything else to her as the store began to empty out leaving the both of them waiting, scrolling away at their phones before a new batch of hungry customers made their way in. The scent of his cologne tickled her nostrils, bothering her because she had never smelled the heavenly fragrance before. She loved men's cologne. She'd go into to Macy's just to sniff the men's fragrances and even used to take late night shower's in Axe body wash in high school when she missed male comfort, though she'd never admit it. She was stupid at sixteen, but who the hell wasn't? This scent though, was different and it almost made her mouth water. Nothing was better than a good smelling man.

She turned to compliment him on the slight scent of bitter orange and vanilla as an apology for her annoyance which probably wasn't even a big deal. She loved when a man smelled nice without it having to be a special occasion. His scent was as subtle as body wash but still smelled great nonetheless. Turning to face him though, she got a good glimpse of him. She hated to describe very dark skin as chocolate, but she'd be lying if she said his skin didn't look like an unwrapped Hershey bar.

His face was flawless and blemish free and his lips didn't even hold a bit of pink. His hair, jet black and silky, sat

34

on top of his head in a low cut with spinning waves. Only seconds before, she thought that you couldn't get any better than a great smelling man, but dammit if the man in front of her didn't scream perfection from head to toe. His great taste in cologne had to be an added bonus. *"Jesus Christ,"* she thought to herself as her eyes danced around every feature he had to offer, from his almond shaped eyes to his full lips, and the neatly tapered beard he sported.

His white t-shirt clung to his bulky arms as he outstretched one to grab the bag of food that Dakota didn't realize belonged to her. She had seemed to lose power in her ears and her voice, only utilizing her eyes to size him up. "This is yours." He told her in a low deep voice as he handed it to her before grabbing his own.

"Thank you." She said snapping out of the slight trance she had been in.

"Good night." He told her before leaving out of the building with his phone glued to his ear.

Noticeably embarrassed, Dakota swiped a piece of hair behind her ear and took her bag to a nearby table to eat in instead of risking her food getting cold on the walk back home in the cool, night time weather. The store had emptied out rather quickly and once Dakota noticed the young woman come around to wipe things down, she knew that they would be closing soon.

"I'm sorry. I didn't even realize it was so late already and you were closing." She said as she began to pack her food back into the bag.

"Oh no, you're fine. I'm just making sure nobody else makes their way in here." She said as she grabbed a small bowl of cabbage and a beef patty for herself. "Shit, I'm hungry too. You mind if I sit?"

Dakota chuckled and shook her head before sticking a forkful of cabbage in her mouth. What else did she have to do besides sit alone with the owner of the Jamaican restaurant she was eating from? "You don't come here often, huh?" the young woman across from her asked in a heavy accent that let her

36

know that either she or her parents weren't originally from the states.

"No, not really," Dakota admitted. "This wasn't here before I left for school, I don't think." She said taking another look around.

"Maybe not. We've been here for about three years. Not too long. But you graduated? Congratulations! That's big!" the young woman said as if they weren't just meeting for the first time. She was outgoing for sure and could befriend anyone, anywhere. Koko found that admirable. She'd never initiated a conversation with a stranger, which was probably why she didn't have many friends.

"No, I actually just decided I was finished," Dakota informed slightly embarrassed for the second time in minutes. Here this woman was looking to be in the same age bracket as her with her own business and she couldn't even make it through undergrad.

"I always wanted to go to school, but I was destined for other things." She said signaling for the small restaurant.

"Girl, please! School for what when you're already a successful business owner? I would love to be in your shoes." Koko admitted and they both shared a heavy laugh that echoed through the empty building.

"I'm Akira by the way." She said extending her hand for Dakota to shake. Even with her full hair up in a messy bun and her rocking an Adidas tracksuit, she was still very pretty.

"Koko." Dakota returned the gesture before placing a plantain into her mouth and groaning in satisfaction. With her eyes shut temporarily to savor the flavors, the sight of the chocolate guy from not even an hour before flashed beneath her eyelids. His solid white tee shirt clashing with the dark hue of his skin sent her through a world of euphoria.

"Do you know that guy who was in here earlier?" Dakota asked before she could stop herself.

Akira squinted her eyes slightly and raised her brow as if she were sizing her up making Dakota's eyes widen. "Wait, is he your boyfriend?" she wondered, feeling like an idiot, but when Akira chuckled she sighed internally of relief.

"Girl hell no. He's like my brother. Why? You want me to throw you the oop?" she asked with a smirk, wondering if Dakota wanted her to introduce the two.

"Oh no. No. I was just" she paused before sticking her fork into the last of her cabbage. "Making conversation."

"It's funny, I've never been good at making friends with other women," Akira admitted truthfully. Even with her bubbly, outgoing personality she had grown up the boujie princess of her family being the only woman with the exception of her mother. She had friends in Jamaica, but upon moving to the states she found that bitches were too fraudulent for her thorough demeanor. "But you're cool, Koko. And I'm really good at reading people. It's one of the gifts I possess," She laughed causing Dakota to follow suit.

"Here, take my number and we can go shopping or something?" Dakota asked hesitantly like she was waiting for a rejection to a date.

"Definitely," Akira exclaimed, and just like that, a friendship was born. *It was a blessing and a curse.*

FIVE

• • •

Monday's were usually Trinity Atkins' longest, most drawn out days, so she sighed of relief once she stepped out of the science building of her school. It was the time of year where the school had the air on but it wasn't quite summertime yet and the air outside proved it. "I don't understand why it's freezing inside and damn near freezing outside. When the hell am I supposed to get some relief?" she huffed into her headphones and listened to her sister laugh in response. "Trini world problems." Ivy joked. Her sister was dramatic and had been since they were children which is why Ivy had seemingly trademarked the slogan for her.

She had just finished her last class of the day and couldn't wait to get home to an empty house and hop into her bed. It was only two in the afternoon, but she had been on campus since eight that morning and knew that it would take her damn near an hour to get back home on the bus. Her toxicology courses always seemed to be in the mornings and she wouldn't dare skip no matter how tired she was, since that was her major.

"If I would've known you were going to move out and just be stuck in your apartment not doing shit, I would've told you to leave me your car," Trinity said causing Ivy to chuckle yet again.

"Trini, please. First of all, you can't even drive. And second of all…no bitch!" she finished after a slight pause that made Trinity roll her eyes.

Trini and Ivy were two completely different people. Trinity knew that if she had Ivy's means of transportation she would utilize it way better than her boring sister. "Talk to mommy and daddy. You know they'll get your spoiled ass a car. You're a good kid and make good grades-"

Ivy's words went in one ear and out of the other as Trini eyed her surroundings. The weather was cool so there was an abundance of dudes sporting Timberlands and hoodies out that it made her mouth water. She was a sheltered kid who was only expected to date pastor's kids or the son's or grandsons of other church members, but hood niggas were her weakness. A horn honking snapped Trinity out of her thoughts and she quickly crossed the street before the light changed. To her surprise though, she continued to hear beeping before a midnight blue Maserati parked beside her. She had never seen one in person, but she'd know the signature trident logo anywhere.

"Yeah, I'm getting rid of it now. Let me call you right back." She heard the driver mumble as he hopped out of the car and approached her.

He wasn't tall, only about three inches taller than her standing at about five feet eight inches, but height was the last thing he needed. Everything else about him was intriguing enough. The fresh "butters" he sported went well with his denim distressed jeans and olive green bomber jacket. She found herself staring so hard that she bumped right into him, sending her textbook and cell phone flying right to the concrete. Trinity knew that the guy standing before her had to be bad news just by the hard, steel that poked her once she had bumped him because she knew it wasn't his dick. It had to be a gun, but the slight smirk that tugged at his lips revealed dimples in his cheeks had her mesmerized.

He extended his hand to help her up off the ground and she got a whiff of whatever it was he had showered with. "My fault, ma." He apologized before picking up her cracked phone and disheveled book.

"Fuck!" Trinity yelled as she snatched the phone from him, careful not to cut herself on the cracked screen. A cracked screen was the last thing she needed when she was trying to prove that she was responsible to her parents, who had just gotten her that phone. With her being a full-time student, her parents expected her to put her all into her studies. They felt as though she didn't need to work, but she wasn't trying to give them any unnecessary expenses. Especially when she was trying to get a car out of them.

"Did I do that?" the mystery guy before her wondered but at that moment he was the last thing on her mind.

"I have to go."

"Wait. Wait, hold on." He called as she proceeded to walk away. His slight grasp on her wrist sent a wave of electricity through her body; *specifically her lady parts*.

"Let me get it fixed for you." He suggested and Trinity scoffed.

"Is that your way of trying to tell me you're a nigga with money? If so, it wasn't attractive."

His roar of laughter caught her by surprise showcasing the braces that adorned his perfectly straight, white teeth. "If I wanted to impress you with some money you think I'd offer to pay sixty dollars to fix an iPhone screen? That's light sweetheart. Give me a little more credit than that."

"I can't give you any credit. I don't know you." She told him, attitude apparent in her voice. The way he swiped his tongue over his bottom lip and smirked as if he felt challenged intrigued her. But the way he grabbed onto her wrist slightly and pulled her toward his car enchanted her. She knew she should've turned her happy ass around and made her way to

44

the bus stop, but for some reason, she didn't feel threatened. She felt safe.

The inside of his car was even more impressive than the outside. It looked like it had come straight from a magazine cover or commercial. The new car scent masked with the smell of something fruity caught Trini's attention. "This must be your mother's car. Or your girlfriend." She observed and watched his cheeks rise as he laughed at her yet again. She had never had a thing for men with braces, but the more he smiled, the more she thought maybe she was missing out.

"Every nigga's car has to smell like black ice or some shit, huh?" He wondered as he quickly glanced over at her. "That shit makes my eyes burn." Trinity found herself chuckling slightly and taking in the mystery guy's features.

His skin was bronzed, his eyelashes long and beautiful like the falsies she sported and his light brown freckles lightly covered his nose and cheeks. He looked so innocent but so bad at the same time.

"How old are you?" She asked causing him to turn and face her at the red light. She was only nineteen and was hoping she wasn't riding in the car with a thirty-year-old man, even though he didn't look to be a day over twenty-one. The slight tilt of his head and furrow of his brows made her raise her brows as well wondering if she had offended him.

"That's the first thing you want to know about me? My age? You don't want to know my name?"

He pulled up in front of a small electronic store that fixed smartphones as well other gadgets for the low and parked. He extended his hand for Trinity's phone and she reluctantly placed it inside, but not before uttering a small "I'm Trinity." to him. His response was simple.

"Risen." His tone held so much power even as he spoke his name that made her want to know more about him. Way more than how old he may have been.

"Risen," Trinity repeated out loud as she watched him walk around to the back, pop the trunk and quickly toss something inside, then look both ways before entering the store as if he were crossing the street. She wasn't in a neighborhood she was too familiar with, and him checking his surroundings should've worried her and made her hop her ass out and onto the bus that was only up the street. *There's still time to get out of here, Trini. Just say you lost the phone.* The angel on her shoulder reminded and she could see the bus stopping at the stop behind her. But something about him captivated her, so she let the devil win.

Trini bit down on her lip and quickly dug into her oversized tote and coated her lips with gloss and smoothed down the hair of the two French braids she wore, unsure of what she looked like after a long day of classes. "You don't have to do all that. You look good." She heard from beside her and realized Risen had made his way to her side of the car and into the rolled down window.

"Shit." She huffed as she dropped her lip gloss onto the floor by her feet.

"You have to be more mindful of your surroundings sweetheart." He smirked before walking around to his side of the car and sliding in. He was clearly a charmer, she could already tell. "So, Trinity. It'll be a little while before your phone is fixed. You mind if I get to know you a little while we wait?"

"And what if I do mind?"

"Then, no disrespect, but you can go inside and wait for your shit and I can be on my way." He reminded causing Trinity to tilt her head a little. "I'm a busy man."

The petty in her wanted to hop out of the car even though she was curious to know a little more about him, simply because she felt tried. But she didn't.

"First of all, nigga, you clearly aren't that busy if you could stop what you were doing to get my phone fixed and still wanted to spend more time getting to know me." She informed with a neck roll.

"Well, I take care of my responsibilities. I was partially responsible for your broken phone, so I took care of it. And I make time for things I want to make time for. And since you didn't get your ass up and leave, you might as well save all of

48

that neck rolling and shit." He told her forcing a smirk to tug at her lips.

"How old are you?" She asked again and watched him slouch back a little.

"Just turned twenty. What about you?"

"Nineteen." She admitted, slightly embarrassed that they were nearly the same age and he was driving around in a new foreign car and dropping money on people he had just met while she barely had sixty dollars to her name. "What do you do?" she asked him and felt a shiver at the look she received in return.

"I ain't no good." He admitted, wanting to get it out in the opened before anything between them went further than their initial conversation. She was beautiful to him for sure, which was why he had stopped to talk to her after watching her walk across the street. Trinity's chestnut tone and honey blonde tresses were enough for him to pull over, but he was finding himself enjoying her feisty personality too. "But I'm a good nigga if that makes sense."

Surprisingly to her, it did make sense and she was curious to see for herself exactly what that meant.

SIX

. . .

Cash checked the time as he found himself stuck in traffic knowing that he was running late. Meek Mill's Wins and Losses album blasted through the speakers of his candy apple red c-class Mercedes Benz, but not too loud. The last thing he needed was to be pulled over simply because he was a nigga who liked rap music and could afford his vehicle of choice.

There was so much that he needed to do, but his mother was big on mandatory weekly dinners so he was on his way to meet his brother, and older sister at their parents' suburban home.

Often times people would associate Cash and Caine with hoodlums who had no father and an absent mother growing up based off of what they did for a living, but that was far from the truth. Sure, they were from the hood but they grew

up with both their mother, father and older sister, Chyna.
Legacy, their father, wasn't a street nigga. But he a hustler
nonetheless. As they were growing up, they noticed that their
father would always find a way to provide for his family and
made sure they lived comfortably. Whether it was legally or
illegally, he got shit done. And while some didn't approve of
some of his tactics, including their older sister who wasn't his
biological child, his twin boys found it admirable.

"Cash." His brother greeted once he stepped foot into
the spacious home and took in the scent of pot roast in the
oven. He'd know the smell anywhere since it was his favorite.

"Keep that Cash shit at the door, Cassim." His mother
scolded.

"That wasn't even me." Cash reminded and she gave
him a look that showed him that she didn't really care. She
loved her boys and supported them, but always found a way to
show them that she didn't approve of everything that they did.

"You too Cairo. Leave Caine at the door."

"They're just nicknames, Celeste. Nobody's telling you to leave Chink at the door." Their dad said speaking up in their defense only to receive a neck roll from their mother.

"You like Chink though." She mumbled flirtatiously and Caine playfully turned to walk back out.

"I'm not about to deal with this today." He said forcing immediate laughter in the Evans home. The three of the siblings admired how their parents loved one another. They were the perfect example of how a man was supposed to treat a woman and how a woman was supposed to treat her man in their eyes.

Chyna scoffed slightly, making her presence known in true Chyna fashion. She cringed at even the thought of yet another conversation about her brothers' career choices. She never hesitated to let it be known that she didn't agree, even when no one asked her or cared for her opinion on the matter. Her six-month pregnant belly protruded as she walked from the kitchen to the dining room with a clear baking dish filled with roast, carrots and potatoes to go along with the mac and cheese, fresh green beans and biscuits. It was a lot for a Thursday evening, but they appreciated a home cooked meal from their mother on any day of the week.

"Chyna why must you always have to be the one to ruin the moment? Can we not start the day like this?" Caine asked with a sigh, being the only one to feel the negativity radiating off of her so quickly. Chyna's chuckling only confirmed it for him.

"Like you really give a fuck, Cairo. "

Chyna Lewis was four years her twin brothers' senior and at twenty-nine she didn't hesitate to remind them of what she thought they should be doing. In her eyes, she was supposed to be the model child. She was a college graduate and worked from sun up to sun down in an office setting in one of the large skyscrapers that you could see from any part of the city. She was engaged to be married and a mother of one three-year-old daughter and a brewing son. Yet still, somehow she seemed to be the odd child.

Chyna was three when her mother had met Legacy and while she had always viewed him as her father figure there was no denying that she wasn't born of his blood. He and both her brothers shared a dark chocolate skin tone while she was fair toned that reddened in the bitter cold weather. Her eyes were big and bold with a hue of hazel while everyone else in her home possessed dark brown orbs. She was always presumed to be beautiful and she knew that she was, but it didn't take away that she didn't look like anyone else in her house. Not even their mother even though she was a redbone herself. Her eyes were chinky and dark, almost black like her long tresses.

The older she got, and the closer her family got the more left out she felt. Her mother was married with two boys made of love and her husband's blood, while Chyna began to feel like a red-headed stepchild. Although she was biologically her mother's daughter, and she and her brothers shared the same blood, she felt like she didn't belong in their family dynamic. She didn't even know her father. Shit, she wasn't even sure if her mother knew her father.

"Chyna stop acting like a fucking brat and grow up." Caine huffed, growing annoyed with his sister already after only a few minutes. He was the only one who couldn't ignore her dramatics. He was sick of hearing about her fake problems every week.

His annoyance with her stemmed from his anger. He and Chyna were always close. All three of them were, but Chyna's unnecessary insecurities ruined the bond they once had. She began to separate herself and try to blame the family for it.

"I need to grow up? I am grown. Y'all need to grow up and get real jobs." She began as she sat at the table before everyone else. "You would think that was something your parents would tell you but-"

"I didn't say anything to you, therefore you need to leave *y'all* out of your rebuttal, beloved," Cassim announced sternly as he scrolled through messages on his phone not bothering to look up at his older sister. "And by the way, if we want to get technical. I have a degree too and still make more money than you so what are you getting at?" he finished, finally looking up and staring at her.

"That's enough." Legacy's voice boomed. While it was clearly no secret that he wasn't Chyna's biological father, he had cared for her since she was a toddler and she knew even in anger she had to respect him for that, especially in his home. "Now I'm not sure what your issue really is, but it's getting really old and tiring. You can sit down and enjoy family dinner with some decent conversation or we can see you next week."

"Who is my father?" She almost yelled directing her attention to their mother and Cash chuckled.

"This is a joke, right? You're almost thirty let it go." He wondered as Legacy stood.

"I'm your father." He reminded, hurt and anger apparent in his tone. His work shirt clung to his muscular frame and his facial hair was neatly groomed making it noticeable that he was indeed the twins' father. It was probably the same reminder that made Chyna feel the same way every time she went home to her parents'.

"My real father." She mumbled, her voice slightly shaky as she looked around the table where everyone sat, eyeing her like the disappointment she always felt like.

"I am your real father! You want to put all of your energy into a nigga who didn't want you and want to give me your ass to kiss like I wasn't there? You disrespect me and your mother, your brothers and this house every time you step foot in it. Father or not, grown or not, the next time even the smallest, slickest remark comes out of your mouth my foot will be up your ass, Chyna."

The table fell silent as Cash reluctantly stuck his fork into the dish and retrieved a few potatoes to put on his plate. His mother stared at him with squinted eyes as if they weren't already chinky enough.

"Listen, I didn't eat all day waiting for this dinner. I'm starving. Chyna's dramatic ass is being typical Chyna and I'm hungry, mom." He pouted but slightly lightened the heavy tension surrounding them. He was the baby by sixty-two seconds and Chink treated him as such, allowing him to get away with almost anything.

"Sorry, daddy." Chyna mumbled as tears trickled down her cheeks. "I love you, I'm just." She paused. "Cairo and Cassim look just like you. There's no denying you're their father. I have a daughter who looks just like me and I have no idea who I even look like." She finally admitted sadly. "But I don't mind being the cute one out of these two." She smiled, wiping her eyes. Her new pregnancy had made her more hormonal and emotional than ever, and the thought of brining another child into the world who looked like her but not her family saddened her.

"Shut your bipolar ass up." Cash chuckled slightly as they finally began to make plates and begin the dinner portion of their family dinner.

Caine's cell phone rang not long after the small talk began and Cash got a glimpse of the name floating across the screen as Akira. Caine quickly silenced his phone and stood, stuffing it in his pocket as if it weren't ringing. He excused himself and made his way out to the porch while Cash scrunched up his face in slight confusion. He watched his mother smirk as she began to pile food onto her husband's plate.

By the time Caine returned almost a half hour later, his plate had gotten cold and his parents and siblings were engulfed in laughter and conversation, which was the point of the weekly dinners. He had been gone a bit longer than expected and once he saw that everyone had begun to enjoy desert, Celeste's cheesecake, he felt bad. "Sorry, mom." He said as he sat back in his seat at the table. "That was business."

"Boy don't you ever sit in my face and lie to me for no reason. Did I ask you who you were out there talking to?" She scolded. Lying was one of the only things that they still got scolded for. It was one reason why Cash hated being lied to so much. He got it honestly from his mother.

Chyna snickered like they were still children as she stood to retrieve her light jacket from the back of the chair letting it be known that she would be the first to go. "Good night everybody. I have to get home and get ready for work in the morning. I'll make sure to bring Mia and Marcus next week." She assured before giving her father a warm, apologetic hug, etching a note in her head to talk to him later. "Love you, daddy."

"I love you too, baby. Good night."

Standing in between the twins, Chyna wrapped one arm around each of them as she pulled them into her. She talked her shit to them, but that's what older siblings were for. And even though she didn't care for a lot of the things they did, she definitely loved her brother's. "I love y'all. Be safe."

Celeste bid her daughter adieu and wrapped up Caine's food simultaneously at his request as their family dinner began to end. The Roman numerals on the large wall clock revealed that it was well after ten at night and Legacy still woke up early every morning for work as well.

"I love you, mom," Cassim said as he kissed her cheek and dapped up his father.

He had left out, knowing that his twin was about to get cursed out by their mother as if he were twelve instead of twenty-five. "Hey," he called to his sister as she made her way to the driver's side of her car. "Call me if you need me." She smiled up at him and guaranteed that she would before she drove off into the night leaving Cash to his own thoughts. The cool, late night wind hit him and he breathed in the crisp air. It smelled different there. Not like the nasty blend of piss and cigarette smoke. It smelled fresh, like earth. Trees, grass, wood, and rain. It was refreshing to him. Even the silence was invigorating, although he was definitely a city boy. It made him believe that everything he had done to get his parents here was worth it.

Caine met his brother on the porch with furrowed brows. They had driven separate cars, but Cash stood before him with his hands in his pockets as if he were waiting for him. Taking his hands out of his pocket, he folded them across his chest.

"You good? That phone call lasted a little minute."

"Yeah, that was just Riz talking about some shit." He flagged and Cash's forehead scrunched in confusion and frustration.

"You're moving funny, bro."

"What, nigga?" Caine asked, stepping closer out of habit. Disrespect was something that he didn't tolerate and he was feeling disrespected by his brother's words.

"You're lying and shit. Even to me? If I can't trust you, who the fuck am I supposed to be able to trust?"

"Man, you tripping off of a phone call that I received that didn't concern you? Everything I do is not going to concern you, bro."

Cash chuckled. "You think I give a fuck about that shit? It's a lot that you do that doesn't concern me. But you lying to me," he said, slapping his chest as he spoke the last word. "That's some shit that's not cool and doesn't sit well with me. Real shit. If you're fucking Akira, fuck her but don't lie to me."

Caine mirrored his brother's stance and folded his arm over his chest unsure of what to say next. Truthfully, he didn't want his brother to know about Akira simply because he wasn't the type to be tied to one girl; however, Akira had him acting in ways he wasn't used to. He was slightly embarrassed by it. Embarrassed by the fact that he was no longer in control of his feelings.

He didn't expect anyone to find out. Especially since he was so low key, but this was his twin brother he was talking about. They knew one another better than they knew themselves for the most part.

"So what you want to fight me because I'm getting some consistent pussy now?" Caine joked causing Cash to laugh loudly.

"Fuck you, lying ass nigga. Now y'all can stop making googly eyes at each other at every damn meeting." He said walking away.

Caine, not able to let Cash walk away with the last word laughed and caught up to him as he was preparing to step food into his freshly washed beamer. "Don't be mad at me because you haven't had a woman since high school."

"I don't need a woman to get pussy." Cash reminded and Caine nodded unable to argue with him there.

"Good, your ass is too soft for these women anyway. They'd have you whipped and unfocused real quick." He joked.

"Fuck you. Let me know when you get home." Cash huffed before peeling off leaving Caine chuckling behind him.

Twenty-five wasn't old at all, but Cash often felt way older. The things that excited a lot of those in his age range didn't excite him too much. He wasn't boring, but he didn't drink or smoke like most. His brother, on the other hand, was a party animal. He'd go out every night if he could. He hated to sit still while Cash found solace in being in the house, watching movies. That might explain why he hadn't been anything more than physically attracted to anyone. His best bet was to get a cougar if he ever wanted to find love, but that was the farthest thing from his mind anyway.

SEVEN

• • •

The living room reeked of fresh laundry along with the shepherd's pie and cornbread Zimora had made for dinner. She hated the meal, but it was her husband's favorite. She was really exhausted and knew the laundry could wait until the next day since it would start the weekend, but she didn't want to hear Marcus' mouth. Especially after the day they had yesterday.

Arguing and fighting daily got so exhausting that she would rather tire herself out making sure that the house was spotless so that he had nothing to complain about. But he always found something. The front door opened, trailing in a temporary blast of unusual nighttime summer like heat and Marcus waltzed in taking off his burgundy scrub top to reveal the tank top underneath.

His job as a registered nurse was demanding during the day, so she understood him always being tired once he got home.

"Are you hungry?" Zimora asked as she made her way to where he stood for a proper greeting.

"What'd you cook?"

Would that determine whether or not you're hungry? She thought to herself but didn't dare vocalize it. Then she'd have to hear his mouth and she just wanted to go to bed.

"Shepherd's pie."

"I'll take it for lunch. I'm just going to get a bowl of cereal." He suggested and Zimora pursed her lips together.

"Oh okay." She said, leaving the silence and awkwardness behind her as she headed for the bathroom. It was after eleven and way past her self-proclaimed bedtime, but she knew a shower would put her right out.

Steam from the shower crowded the bathroom like smoke from a blazing building and relief washed over Zimora in the form of hot water. She could feel the kinks in her back and shoulders washing away with the suds of her Olay body wash. However, she felt them reappear once Marcus stepped in behind her.

They washed in silence and just before Zimora went to step out, Marcus held a firm grip on her inner thigh, something that used to turn her on. He bit his plump lip as he eyed her dripping wet milk chocolate skin with lust. "Damn, look at you." He said palming her ass to pull her closer, letting the water rain down her back. She wasn't really in the mood. But this was her husband and he wasn't the understanding type.

Wrapping her arms around his neck, she allowed the peck he intended to be planted on her lips to graze the side of her mouth and ignored his confused glare. It was no secret that the love they once shared wasn't the same. She played her part, obviously but it was his lack of communication, controlling spirit, anger issues, and sneakiness that brought it about in her eyes. And there was, of course, their physical altercations that would put the icing on any cake. Still, though, he was her husband.

Not in the mood for foreplay, Zimora reached down to stroke the swollen member between his legs, leaning in closer to him so that his back rested against the cool shower wall and away from the water. Her lips stayed connected to his neck as she felt him harden in her hands. His groaning made her suck a little harder but he quickly moved his head and smirked down at her. "You must be ready for me." He flirted as he swiped his finger over her entrance to see how wet she was. "Shit."

Marcus loved Zimora. They had been through a lot together, but it never made him love her any less even though sometimes he didn't pick the best ways to show it. He knew that he wasn't always the best husband and maybe wasn't even ready to be anyone's husband so soon, but that ship had sailed. He was only twenty-nine and twenty-seven when he said I do while the majority of his friends were still in their bachelor stages of life. He was in love, so he didn't care at first, but hanging with them showed just how different their lives were and he missed it. And while he found himself in situations he shouldn't have been in as a married man, he was still that. A married man and he knew that he and his wife had to make it work. He was sure that they could.

The two lovers switched places, and Zimora's back on the cool shower wall mixed with the steam around her made her nipples harden in arousal and anticipation. Marcus noticed and latched his mouth around one while fondling the other with his hand. Exhaustion was the last thing on her mind as she tilted her head back and let her body relax and accept the enjoyment. "Mmm." She moaned, feeling her body get lifted slightly and her legs widen and she knew that finally, it was time.

Zimora was already melting before he had even gotten all the way in. Marcus was a lot of things, but a bad lover wasn't one of them. He could definitely sling some good dick. And him being a moaner didn't make things better for her. It was the sexiest thing she had ever heard pass his lips second to "I love you" and "I do."

His slow strokes quickened as she held onto his neck for dear life so that neither of them would slip. Marcus stood at five, eleven with small, jet black curls resting on top of his head. His full beard was neatly trimmed with eyes filled with lust. For a second she didn't see the angry, controlling Marcus. She saw the handsome manly man she had fallen in love with and it made her wrap her legs around his waist and gently claw at his back. His heavy breathing in her ear earned hummed moans into his as she allowed her body to relax completely to enjoy her man.

"Shit." He huffed in frustration as he almost snatched the shower curtain off the rod to get them out of the shower. Zimora giggled at his attempt to keep them both steady and not slip on the wet floor. She knew that he had grown impatient in the shower and was going to finish in their king sized bed. She had no complaints.

Zimora crawled onto the bed, sinking into the white sheets and she stretched her body out like a cat, leaving only her ass in the air. "Damn, girl." Marcus groaned and Zimora earned a loud slap that actually hurt, but she knew the pleasure was soon to follow. With both cheeks palmed in his hands, he entered his wife from behind.

It was moments like those when he remembered why he married her. She was everything to him, and still managed to have the best pussy he had ever had. He slid his hands up her back and into her hair as he pounded into her. Marcus snatched the ponytail out of her hair and roughly pulled her up and into him, knowing she loved that shit. His lips tickled her ear and he wrapped his hand around her neck gently, and her body slightly tensed up.

Zimora pulled his hand off of her neck, having her pleasure be replaced with images of bad memories. "Are you going to have my baby?" He asked in between heavy breaths. He was about to cum and she hoped he didn't ruin it for himself or her. Marcus didn't realize that his wife was on birth control to purposely avoid having his child. Their relationship was toxic and definitely not what she would want to bring a child into. She feared it. But telling him that would only bring about more toxicity and proven points.

She moaned louder, but that didn't make him ignore the question like she had hoped. "Huh, baby? You going to have my baby?" The way his hands gripped her hips and he breathed out, let her know that he was about nut and was praying that he did it before she was forced to answer. She could have easily said yes and allowed him to dump in her knowing she was on birth control anyway, but she couldn't bring herself too. She believed that even saying yes would miraculously get her pregnant even with the birth control and she didn't want to risk it.

Their climax came at once and once their heavy breathing ceased the space around them grew thick with tension. Not bothering to ask the question again, Marcus stood and put a pair of basketball shorts on over his underwear and slipped his feet into a pair of Nike slides.

"Are you going somewhere?" Zimora asked only for her words to fall on deaf ears. He was pissed, and when he was pissed he didn't think like a married man. More like a high school boy. Ignoring her, he slipped a tank top over his head

74

and left out slamming both the bedroom door and the front. Zimora sighed and tossed her head back onto the fluffy pillowcase. It was well after midnight, and she didn't have time to care at that point. She had to work in the morning.

Marcus, on the other hand, had nothing but time since he worked over night. Well, at least in *Chyna's* eyes. Zimora Freeman was Marcus' wife. The person who shared his last name, but Chyna Lewis was his girl. They had been together longer than he had even been married. Chyna didn't realize that she was only his side chick though. Or in this case, his mistress. He had gifted her with a ring to express his love for her once she had birthed their daughter, Mia. Mia was an unexpected blessing but Marcus knew the moment he found out Chyna was pregnant that he had gotten in way too deep with her. Now here he was about to have another child by her and his wife still didn't want to carry one for him. Luckily for Mark, Chyna hadn't pressured him about a wedding date, and hopefully, she wouldn't because he had no true intentions of marrying her.

All of the lights were off once he stepped foot in his other home. The sweet smell of Chyna's pink sand candles tangoed the aroma of chicken Parmesan she had made for dinner. Mia's television in her bedroom quietly hummed the tunes of the Trolls soundtrack and Marcus smiled. Zimora didn't know about Chyna obviously, or the blessing and a half that they shared. It would crush her. It would break her and Marcus would never have the heart to tell her. He was in way too deep. He had his wife on one hand and the mother of his children on the other. And his relationship with both depended on the relationship with the other.

The bedroom door creaked opened and Chyna quickly sat up and eyed her man's silhouette as he stood in the doorway. "Babe? What are you doing here? I thought you left for work already."

"Yeah, they actually canceled me for the night. I go in tomorrow morning now. So I can lay with you and my boy tonight." He mumbled into her neck.

"Good. We missed you, daddy." She giggled. Too tired to entertain much more conversation after the work he had put into blowing his wife's back out, he only pecked her cheek in response.

I know she's sleeping well tonight. Ass naked more than likely He thought to himself before biting his lip at the thought then quickly shaking it off as Chyna turned to face him.

"I love you, babe. I can't wait to be your wife." She smiled and he could tell even in the darkness.

"I love you too. Goodnight." He hummed, feeling bad. He would never tell her that she was dodging a bullet by not being his wife. He wasn't worth shit and he knew it.

EIGHT

• • •

"So, do you like niggas from North? Or uptown?"
Akira asked, watching the loud bus let a crowd of passengers
of at the corner stop only to fill it right back up with more.
"That can't really be a question." Koko chuckled. "North side
niggas for sure. They're just different. They move different,
walk different, talk different. Everything." She gushed before
giggling. "Or I could just be biased."

In only a few weeks, spring had left and was replaced
by hot summer like days. Dakota and Akira sat side by side on
the stoop of an abandoned house as the hot concrete slightly
burnt the skin of their thighs as they both sported short shorts.
Even Dakota was surprised that upon exchanging numbers with
Akira that they had actually kept in contact.

"Yeah biased because of your new nigga," Akira joked,
but Koko quickly shut her down.

"Don't even say it." She laughed. "You keep trying to make me like that man and I keep telling you I don't even know him. You're allowed to see someone and think they're attractive without plotting on them. He's attractive. That's it, that's all. Don't make something out of nothing."

"Yeah okay," she said with an eye roll letting it be known that she didn't believe a thing that had come out of Koko's mouth.

"Who's attractive?" the sound of his profound tone seemed to only be heard in Koko's dreams so to hear it beside her made her whip her head into his direction.

Children ran down the sidewalk chasing the ice cream truck before the song it played traveled too far down to catch. Their school uniforms and book bags still clung to some proving that they hadn't made it home yet although it was well after six in the evening. It was a beautiful day and even with how observant she was, she couldn't take her eyes off of him. His face held little emotion, but the gleam in his eyes showed that he knew she found him appealing and he was enjoying it.

"Why are you popping up on me?" Akira asked and Koko was grateful to have his eyes off of her.

"Why aren't you answering your phone?" He asked and the gleam in his eyes quickly disappeared. Unbeknownst to Koko, he was in business mode and Kira quickly sat up, pulling her phone from her pocket to see that it had died. Immediately she stood, growing annoyed with herself. She knew she needed to stay accessible and hated the idea of missing something because she had been slipping. It was crazy having to always be on go, even when trying to enjoy the day and be a regular young adult. Cash noticed and smiled small. "Relax, my mom just wanted to see you. And stop bringing people to my house," he mumbled as he looked around before walking inside what seemed to be an abandoned building on the outside.

It actually was abandoned in the sense that no one lived there and it was boarded up on the outside, but the inside of the home that Cash and Caine grew up in with their parents and sister was now an office that the twins used every so often. It was low key because it was off the radar and nostalgic because it showed the boys where they had come from and where they had to go. There was only one small desk, a swirling office chair, discreet cameras, a large safe and currency counter. Either Cash or Caine would empty out the safe bi-weekly to stay on top of things, which was why Cash was there. But as he sat to empty out the safe, he noticed Kira and her friend on the small monitor.

He watched Koko toss her head back in genuine laughter at something Akira had said and he found his gaze staying stuck on her a little while longer. Realizing that he was off task, he quickly shook off the smirk tugging at his lips and the thoughts in his head before turning off the monitor and slinging the now heavy book bag he sported over his shoulder. The sun slapped the skin of his face with its rays and forced droplets of sweat to crowd his hairline.

"So what are you doing now that you've left school?" Akira asked her newfound best friend.

"Honestly, I've just been doing hair and makeup until I find a job. I've been putting in applications everywhere it seems like. Either getting a job got harder or I'm applying above my means or something." She admitted, stress laced in her tone.

Akira looked at her and rolled her eyes slightly. They hadn't been friends long at all, but they had definitely grown close in the time that they were. "Girl why didn't you say anything? I can get you a job." She said and looked to Cash who smirked and shook his head before walking off toward the direction of his car.

"No offense, but I love Jamaican food too much to work around it every day and risk getting tired of it." She joked.

"I didn't mean at the restaurant." She laughed. "I know the owner of this bar and they need some pretty bottle girls in there. I can put in a good word for you and the position is yours if you want it."

Koko leaned back against the step above her with her elbows planted on the step as she thought. The sun had begun to hide behind the clouds at the request of their thoughts, leaving the sky gray and the air cooler instantly. The streets seemed to grow deserted quickly of the kids and she looked down at her phone for the time, knowing that soon day would turn into night. She wasn't sure how comfortable she would be parading around a bar at night with very little clothes, but she wasn't really in a position to turn down the opportunity. "Girl yes!" She decided in that moment and Akira smiled. "Thank you."

"We should go tonight!" she said, coming up with the idea for some fun and for her to get used to what would soon be her new work environment. "Chinx is small, but it's cozy and it's popping more on weekdays than weekends in my opinion."

"Tonight?" Dakota asked looking at the time again.

"Yeah, I mean unless you have something better to do with your boring ass." She joked causing Dakota to laugh and roll her eyes.

"Fuck you. I'll go get dressed." She playfully huffed and the two girls dispersed to the directions of their own homes.

Chinx, for lack of better words, was popping just like Akira had expressed it would be. Koko didn't care for clubs, so the cozy little bar with good food and music was right up her alley. And of course, good drinks. Although it was small, it was spacious and definitely more modern that a lot of the little hole in the wall bars she had been to. It was decked in all white from the stools to the bar counter and had just enough overhead light to not be uncomfortably dark. The wall behind the bar was huge and filled with any beverage one could imagine. "Wow, it's really nice in here," Koko observed and Akira nodded proudly.

She remembered when the bar first opened and how it looked nothing like what Koko was complimenting. But the hard work the boys put into it made it come together. Celeste was only a front for the business and a way to give her the cut she would've received regardless of whether she worked there or not. There was no doubt that the bar affectionately named after their mother belonged to the twins, but it gave her something to do nonetheless.

Dressed simply in a strapless white top, denim shorts and classic black and white vans, Dakota felt under dressed compared to Akira who sported a long mustard off the shoulder maxi dress with gold chunky heels. "Girl I wish you would've told me you were really dressing up I wouldn't have worn sneakers," Koko said before ordering a round of Hennessey shots for her and her friend.

"You look fine. I just always dress up when I come. I mean, since I'm one of the managers." She chuckled. "Remind me to get your uniform before we leave."

Dakota's eyes widened, then she snickered before sipping from a pretty drink she had already forgotten the name of. "Real smooth, Kira" Koko joked although she was grateful.

They hadn't even been friends long enough to really consider one another friends, but she was looking out for her more than some of the people she had known for years. Kira opened her mouth to say something but Dakota's peripheral forced her head to the side.

Her heart rate increased as she thought she had to either be tripping or drunk already to be seeing the handsome guy again. Twice in one day. She blinked a few times expecting the mirage of him to disappear, but there he was. Still powerfully leaning against the wall with the lights bouncing off of his skin, peering out at everyone like he owned the place. She quickly looked away and took a sip from her glass, but not before Akira followed her gaze with her own eyes. A smirk tugged at the corners of her mouth. "You like what you see, huh?" She chuckled causing Koko to shift her body nervously. The sober version of Koko could easily shut Kira's assumptions about her wanting her friend down, but the tipsy version of Koko thought she might be on to something. She might not have liked him, but he definitely did something to her every time she saw him.

Knowing the twins for so long, Kira could always tell Cash from Caine. Not only because she had grown an undeniable attraction to Caine, but because Cash was a lot less flashy than Caine. A watch would be his only item of jewelry whereas Caine wore a watch, chain and bottom grills. Cash would sport a crisp solid t-shirt, jeans and finish it off with expensive kicks on his feet.

Noticing her gaze himself, Cash gave Akira a small head nod from across the room and she signaled for him to come over to where she stood. "Bro!" she greeted excitedly as if she hadn't just seen him hours prior. "Sit down and have a drink with my friend and me," Akira suggested knowing that he didn't drink and after a moment of him pondering, he sat and she stood. "I'll be right back."

Dakota scoffed, feeling embarrassed. She knew what Akira was doing but she was making her feel like the friend that had to be set up because they couldn't speak for themselves.

The slight rumble from his laughter made Koko finally look over at him, avoiding his eyes and focusing on his white t-shirt and wondering what he possibly looked like underneath. "You're not a stalker are you? I've been seeing you a lot lately." she wondered, having the liquid courage to be the conversation starter. He chuckled and held up a finger and a bartender brought him a bottle of water immediately. "I would never be that pressed," He answered matter-of-factly before licking his lips. "I heard you were asking about me."

"What? No, not really. I just asked if Akira knew you for the sake of conversation once." She assured.

"Don't ask about me," He told her and she felt intimidated by the seriousness in his face. Suddenly her hands grew clammy, her face warm. She didn't know what to say. But when his mouth opened again to speak, his words weren't what she had expected him to say. "Find out."

He was way too smooth for her liking, and she couldn't allow him to be that smooth all night. "I have a boyfriend." She lied before taking a sip through her straw and was surprised when his rebuttal came immediately after.

"When did I ask you about a boyfriend?"
She was stumped and at a loss for words, so she just stared at him for a second before going back to babysitting her drink.

"Plus, if you had a boyfriend we wouldn't even be having this conversation right now. So either you're lying or unhappy." He said reading through her. "Either way, that's not my business."

Dakota cleared her throat, not wanting to admit to either of his accusations. She stuck her hand out to greet him and was surprised when he smirked and took her hand into his.

"I'm Dakota." She told him.

"Cassim."

NINE

. . .

Trinity's *good as new* iPhone sat on top of her dresser on speaker as she pulled out options for her date night. She and Risen had been talking for a little over a month and had spent a lot of their free time together. And tonight they were finally going on a real first date. It had her completely giddy because she had never been on a real date before.

"He's really cute Ivyana, seriously don't be like that," Trini told her older sister who had jumped into overprotective mode with ease. With her not being around, she felt like she was missing a lot, including things she didn't want to miss. Things like her little sister's first date.

"I'm not worried about how cute he is, just make sure he's good to you," Ivy scolded, sounding like their mother, Isyss. That was the exact reason she hadn't told her parents, now Trini was wondering if it was such a good idea to tell her sister.

Ivy was a goody two-shoes who always followed the rules for the most part. It never usually affected Trini until moments when Ivy forgot that she was her sister instead of their mother.

Riz wasn't Trinity's first boyfriend, but he was the first boyfriend that she could see a future with. She had never envisioned a long-term relationship with anyone, but he was different. He wasn't lying though, when he said that he was no good, but still a good nigga. He claimed that even though he was into street shit, he would be good to her. And thus far, he proved to be a man of his word.

Trinity left the buttons of her red and white baseball jersey undone to show off the white shorts and matching tube top underneath. She wasn't sure where they were going, but she was told to dress comfortable and casual. It excited her that he had actually made plans for her instead of having a debate about where she wanted to go or what she wanted to do.

"Just remember you're only nineteen, Trini. You don't have to rush anything. Boys are like busses. You know, miss one next fifteen one coming."

"Girl if you don't shut your old ass up with these corny phrases and analogies." She fussed slightly. "Have you met anyone yet? Zim told me she's trying to hook you up with one of her clients,"

"I'm working, Trini. That's my focus right now. And why would I want someone who's on trial? Y'all have to stop being so concerned with my love life,"

"Just like you have to stop being so concerned with mine." She hummed as she put a pair of large gold hoops in her ears just before a horn honked outside.

"Is that a horn?" Ivy wondered. "Is that him? That better not be him beeping at you. He better come knock on the door and take you out like a lady!" She huffed and Trini rolled her eyes.

"So daddy can have a heart attack since it isn't Deaconess Johnson's son? Girl please." Trini shrugged as she grabbed her bag and keys.

Trinity bid her parents and her sister adieu all at once before leaving out of the house. The sun beamed down on her and she quickly made her way to Risen's Maserati before her edges could sweat out. Immediately, the scent of Polo Red cologne intoxicated her. It was his favorite and didn't take long to become hers as well.

"Hey ugly." She greeted him with a peck on his lips.

"Now you know." He chuckled against her lips.

Rides from her house to his neighborhood always seemed to be pretty long, but they were always filled with great conversation.

"I don't make you nervous?" he asked before staring straight ahead with his bottom lip pulled between his teeth.

"No. Do you want me to be nervous?"

"No." he laughed. "I just know you're a good girl and shit and probably not used to a nigga like me. I know your

94

parents would shit a brick if they knew you were dealing with me."

"You worry about my parents too much." She giggled, but actually liked that he wanted her parents to like him. It made her believe he really had genuine intentions with her.

"I just hope you're not with me to make your parents upset or something on some white girl rebellious shit."

"I'm black." She chuckled. "But I like what I like. And I like you. That's all that matters to me." She admitted.

"Oh yeah? You like me huh?"

"You know I like you." She flirted, taking in his appearance.

He wore a black and white classic Milano shirt, black distressed jeans and black timberlands as if it wasn't officially summer. Still though, the way black looked on him made her melt. They hadn't had sex yet, but with every day that passed, the anticipation grew. Especially with him looking and smelling the way he did.

"Have you been having sex since we've been talking?" Trinity wondered out loud.

"You sure know how to shift a mood." He huffed like he could already feel like their date would be spoiled before it even began. "No, I haven't fucked anyone lately. I've been too busy if I'm being honest. But until you and I are officially together, I am allowed to." He reminded and Trini sat back in her seat with a pout.

"I mean, I would love to be fucking you. Trust me. But I'm not going to pressure you. I'm also still a man though."

"Well, I appreciate your honesty." She mumbled.

"I would ask if you are, but I don't really want to know the answer if it's not what I want to hear."

"No, I'm not. I only want to fuck you." she pouted, seconds away from a tantrum.

"You want to fuck me so bad that you're about to have a temper tantrum?" He smirked before laughing.

Trinity had to admit that it sounded silly, but her hormones were raging and the thought of him being with anyone but her made her skin grow warm. But the thought of him on top of her in a fit of passion made her lady parts tingle. She had been with a couple of other people before, but it had been a year since her last sexual encounter. She and Ivy had vowed celibacy but now Ivy was still single and lonely and Trini had a man, unofficially. Being in Risen's presence didn't make things better since he made her feel like a wild animal ready to attack.

Sliding her hand over the middle console and into his lap, she groped the front of his jeans and watched him look at her quickly before focusing back on the road. Hesitantly, she undid the button of his pants, then the zipper and before either of them knew it her cool hands were wrapped around the skin of his rising member.

"What you doing?" he asked, shifting his body slightly. She had seen his dick in the nudes she had requested he send her in exchange for her own, but the pictures did him no justice.

"Don't do-" he began but stopped short once Trini's warm mouth wrapped around his dick. "Shit."

Riz parked his car near the grassy area of a park all while Trinity bobbed her head up and down in his lap. She wasn't a pro by any means, but she definitely got an A for effort and Risen was more than pleased. He leaned his seat all the way back and wasted no time pulling Trinity into his lap.

"I know you have a condom." She said matter-of-factly as she kissed his lips, then his neck, while tapping at his pockets.

"Chill," he chuckled, finding her amusing in the moment. "Relax. I'm not trying to fuck you for the first time in the back of a car,"

"I was thinking the front anyway," she hummed, sucking a little harder on his neck and he bit his lip before his infectious laughter filled the car.

"Nah man, come on before I really do it." He said sternly, battling with himself whether or not he really would.

Risen's one weakness was that he was a sucker for love. It could've had a lot to do with the fact that he never had much of it growing up. And while he could surely fuck someone and keep it moving, he had invested time into he and Trini's relationship. So he wanted to make sure she felt how serious he was about her. Pecking her lips, he pulled her closer and rested the palms on his hands on her ass.

"Please stop being a gentlemen for one second," she begged as she grinded in his lap. She discreetly slid the gold wrapped condom from the small compartment on the side of the driver's side door and held it up. "I don't want to wait for the perfect moment. I want to create it." Her words made his dick twitch and he wasted no time attacking her lips with kisses.

The space around them had already begun to grow hot as Riz watched Trinity remove her shirt while he peeled off the one underneath revealing a black strapless bra.

"We have to hurry up babe, we can't sit here too long." Riz mumbled against her neck. He was right, but he couldn't care less about getting caught. He just wanted to hurry up and bury himself deep inside of her.

With their clothes sloppily tossed all over the passenger seat, Trini slid down on his swelling dick, wrapping her arms around his neck. He hissed in satisfaction while biting his lips and watching her eyes roll back in slight ecstasy.

"Damn," he groaned holding onto her hips, helping her bounce up and down slowly.

Trinity buried her head in his neck and began to bounce up and down quicker and Risen's grip on her waist tightened as her moans tickled his ear. He was feeling too soft and wanted to remind her that he was in control, so he lifted her up and slammed her down watching her face ball up in pleasure as she screamed to the ceiling.

"Fuck!"

It had been quite some time for the both of them, but neither of them wanted to be the first to tap out. He continued to guide her movements as his lips attached to the skin of her neck. He had found out early on that it was her spot and it rang true once she tilted her head back, allowing him access to her neck in its entirety. There was so much he wanted to do to her body that he knew he couldn't leave her alone anytime soon.

Even with her eyes shut tightly she could see his face vividly. His smooth skin, light freckles and lust filled eyes. It made her bounce harder as she moaned louder, groping her right breast while his mouth latched to the nipple on the left. Opening them eyes seeing that he was right there in the flesh had her legs to shaking as slapping sounds filled the car. There was no more fight in her. He had done her body good and finally, her body was forcing her release no matter how hard she tried to hold on to it.

"Hold on baby." Riz panted heavily as he slammed her into him repeatedly while she screamed. He was sure that even through the tint anyone in passing could see the foggy windows.

"I can't. I'm-I'm coming." She moaned, now sloppily riding him in a way he couldn't even keep up with.

Trinity accidentally beeped the horn as her head tilted back in bliss. A chill washed over her as she had finally come down from her high. Leaning forward, her eyes met Risen's and she pecked his lips, which turned into yet another make out session.

"Let's get out of here." He mumbled against her lips and she nodded. She raised her body upward off of his now flaccid member and watched him hiss before they began to redress.

"Can you tell me where we're going now?" she wondered as she slid her shorts over her wobbly legs.

"You'll see when we get there." He told her, pulling off while she continued to fix herself. She usually wasn't fond of surprises, but it was cute when it was him who was surprising her.

They arrived at the empty parking lot of a skating rink and even upon entering Trini saw that they were the only ones there.

"There's no one here. I think they're closed." Risen only chuckled. "No, they're not closed." He told her simply and she smirked realizing he had rented the place out just for them. "Nobody's going to see me bust my ass, but I remember you said you used to skate a lot when you were younger.

Trini hit his chest to hide the reddening of her cheeks. "Oh you wait until my legs feel like jello to want to go skating."

"Damn right. If I'm going to be a fall risk, you are too, baby. Show me what you got."

She looked at him and smiled, biting her lips slightly. She was unapologetically smitten and knew that she had no intentions on being with anyone else anytime soon. *Or ever if she could help it.*

TEN

. . .

Dakota stood in the bathroom mirror under the bright overhead lights admiring herself. Her heels clicked against the tile floor as she made sure she had chosen the best shoes to be on her feet all night in. She had to make sure that she was presentable for her first night on the job. She adjusted the black, halter body suit with the name of the bar, *Chinx*, written neatly across the front over her black fishnet tights. She patted her red lips with her middle finger to make sure it was truly matte like advertised and fanned her high lighter brush over her cheekbones, making sure to glow even in the semi dim area.

Tucking her small makeup items into her fanny pack deemed for tips, she swung the door opened. One foot after the other, she quickly stepped out only to stumble then be stabilized by a strong arm that wrapped around her waist. "Look at you looking like you belong." He smirked and she looked up to see Cassim. She smoothed the edges of her bun to keep from accidentally touching his bulky arms on purpose.

Being in his presence didn't make her as nervous since she seemed to bump into him quite often, but there was still something about him that made her shy and act like a little girl.

"You must come here every night, huh?"

"I come here for the seafood." He informed while removing his arm from her waist.

"So you like seafood and Jamaican food, huh?"

"Amongst other things. You trying to figure me out huh?" He mocked and Dakota rolled her eyes playfully.

The occasions when she bumped into him, she got to see that he actually was more than a handsome face that played in her dreams often, as corny as it sounded. He was funny, charming, and they never had a boring or typical conversation. He was someone she looked forward to bumping into. And she always wanted to look presentable just in case, though she'd never admit that.

"I need to get to work. I don't want to be late on my first day." She told him in a slight panic as she eyed the time on her watch.

"Right. You don't want to be late. I heard the owner is a dick." He informed and found amusement in her eyes widening in fright. She went to turn to walk away, but Cassim gently grabbed ahold of her wrist and watched intently as she snapped her head around to look at him. It seemed like it was in slow motion by how quickly he was able to take in all of her features. She looked different. Usually, her face was soft and make up free, showing off her subtle beauty and slightly chubby cheeks. But now she stood before him with what he had learned to be a beat face. The shimmers on her made her glow under the lights and the red tint to her lip drew extra attention to them. She was a beauty for sure, for a lack of better words.

"Call me when you get off?" He asked more so than requested and she nodded feeling her heart skip a few beats.

Finally she thought to herself.

Cassim took Dakota's phone as she extended it to him and put his phone number inside of it, discreetly calling himself to have hers as well. He watched as she quickly traveled across the bar and eased behind the counter. He looked at the time on his twenty-one thousand dollar Audemars Piguet watch before making his way toward the back and out the door. The air was warm to be after ten at night and Cash leaned against the brick wall before eyeing his watch once more.

"Late." He mumbled just before the midnight blue Maserati pulled up. Risen killed the engine immediately and hopped out.

"Traffic," Riz said knowingly once he came face to face with Cash.

"You've been good? I haven't heard from you. I'm trying to make sure that's a good thing." Cash said to his self-proclaimed little brother.

"Yeah, I'm good. Laying low like you said. Plus, I've been hanging with this jawn lately. She's been keeping me occupied."

"Oh yeah? So that's all you needed to calm your ass down a little? Some pussy?"

"Man here you go." Riz chuckled.

"You sure you're good though?"

Cash wanted Risen to know that he cared beyond making sure he was good financially. "Yeah bro, I'm good. You need me for anything tonight?" Cash and Caine didn't deal with day-to-day drug business. They dished product out to whoever was going to sell it and their hands were wiped clean until the next shipment. As far as bagging and selling went, that wasn't their thing. They got their money up front and the rest was up to their customers. "We're good. Enjoy your little friend." He joked, like how his mom used to talk about the significant others of him and his siblings.

"Fuck you." He laughed before making his way back to his car and driving off leaving Cash to enjoy the silence of the night and observe his surroundings for a while longer.

The music was loud and everyone seemed to be enjoying themselves once Cash re-entered Chinx. The scent of food made his stomach rumble as a reminder that he hadn't eaten in hours. He took a seat on the last bar stool on the left and ordered a sprite and the crab cakes that he knew his mother had made and left for him. She only worked during the day. She claimed that the night crowd wasn't for her and she needed to be home with her man at those hours.

Cash ate and watched everyone around him interact like he always did, before finding himself watching Dakota from afar. He saw that she didn't pay any mind to the dudes who tried to grope her or catch her attention as she waltzed around in her heels doing what she had come to do. Work. He was impressed, seeing that they were in an upscale bar filled with niggas who had money. She didn't seem impressed, even as they purposely pulled out wads of cash and black cards to lure her.

Cash felt a presence beside him and quickly turned to see who had made their way into his personal space. He grew surprised to see his twin. There weren't too many times when they were in public places where they could be seen at the same time. Only with blood family, work family, or when it was just the two of them so his pop up had to be important. "I know you're not over here paying attention to the wrong shit," Caine said. "I've been watching you watch this jawn for twenty minutes and I've been watching you miss the fact that there's a Justin Timberlake ass white dude trying too hard to blend in around here."

The JT lookalike caught Cash's eye as soon as the words passed his brother's lips and Caine walked back into the distance out of view, leaving Cash feeling like he had been caught slipping. And the feeling didn't sit well with him.

"Cop." Cash mumbled shaking his head as he too got up to slide out the back before anything suspicious happened.

Caine, who was parked in the back didn't pull off until his brother was safely in his own car and they both drove off in different directions. It was time for them to lay low and keep heat off of the bar. For whatever reason, they were getting hot.

ELEVEN

• • •

Ivy sat on a bench along the disgustingly beautiful Schuylkill River watching bikers and joggers zoom past her. The foot traffic was surprisingly calm in Fairmount Park for it to be a hot summer day, but that could've been because it wasn't even seven in the morning. Detective Gates sat beside her with a large coffee from WAWA in his hand. Personally, she couldn't drink hot coffee on hot days, but she sure had a Dunkin Donuts iced coffee in her own hands. She had grown used to not having to wake up early in the mornings for work so when he called her for a meeting so early, she wished she would have conveniently missed the call.

"So, how's it going? I haven't heard of much progress lately." Detective Gates wondered as he put the cup to his lips and stared straight ahead seemingly in deep thought. He was very attached to the case, but it was something that made him one of the best detectives she knew of.

It had been almost three months since she began her investigation and trying to catch two of Philadelphia's most wanted. Detective Gates had been on her back heavily about the twins and putting more pressure on her than she felt like she needed. If these guys were easy to get, she wouldn't need to go undercover to get to them and he didn't seem to understand that. His main concern was getting them as quick as possible and he made that known from the beginning.

"We're on a time limit, Officer Atkins. The department gave us a year, but I really want to have them sooner. Way sooner. These guys are smart and unpredictable. If you take too long, they'll catch you before you can catch them and then we're screwed." He told her. "Have you worked a case on them before?" Ivy wondered. He seemed to know a lot about them for them to be so secretive.

"No, but I've been around for a long time and I've worked a lot of similar cases." He answered simply.

Dakota wasn't stupid. She knew that Detective Gates' main concern with the case wasn't only her cracking it, but the recognition he would get as well. "I haven't been able to get to the twins yet, but I think I have a lead that'll get me closer. I was sitting outside of my building one night and saw one of the young guys come out. You could tell he was a drug dealer, or whatever he called himself-" she continued before being cut off.

"Ivy, I told you we don't need-"

"Listen, I know. He's a little young corner boy but just listen. I overheard him talking about a guy named Reese who must be higher up. That's where he's getting his product from but Reese has to get drugs from somewhere and I'm almost certain whatever he gets either comes from the twins directly or someone directly under them if he's moving work in the neighborhood I'm staying in.

"Congratulations, Ms. Atkins. You've just figured out something that doesn't matter at all. I don't want to hear anything about the young corner boys, or Reese, or anybody that isn't Cash and Caine. Get me Cash and Caine officer Atkins."

113

Ivyana sighed and stood, feeling tension beginning to brew the longer they sat beside one another. They always had a mutual respect for one another, but now Jonathan was making it a duty to remind her that she was inferior. Feeling borderline defeated and like a failure, she made her way to her car and sat there for a second trying to figure out how she could skip the middleman. Finally, like a light bulb had gone off in her head, a smile spread across her lips. *Just find Reese. Niggas can't resist a pretty woman.* All she would have to do is start a conversation with the young guy from her building asking if he knew where Reese was. If she requested him by name, his young dumb ass would probably assume she did, in fact, know him and give up some information. Then she could get some information on who his suppliers were.

She drove off feeling like a weight had been lifted off of her. Finally, she would be getting somewhere. Checking the time on the car radio, she saw that she was running a bit late for breakfast with her sister and best friend. She wasn't supposed to be combining her two lives, but she missed those who were closest to her.

Trinity and Zimora were already seated at Green Eggs Café, Zim with a cup of coffee and Trinity with an orange juice. "Well, at least you guys waited for me." She said making her presence known.

"Bitch you were taking too long and you know how I love my red velvet pancakes. They were calling me." Trinity assured as she sat back and took a sip of her good source of vitamin c.

"What is this glow you have going on with you?" Ivy wondered reading her younger sister immediately. "You fucked him, huh?" she whisper-yelled and surprisingly Trini didn't try to deny it. She only smirked, unable to hide it. She was sprung.

"Aww is my little baby in love?" Ivy cooed and watched Trinity blush.

"No, not yet. But he is really sweet Ivy! Like, our first date was at the skating rink." She informed, leaving out the part that he had rented the place out just for them. Ivy was her sister, but she was also a cop and she didn't need her digging around in her man's business wondering what he did for a living to be able to afford that luxury. "He listens to me. He confides in me. I feel like we have a real strong connection." She continued, unapologetically smitten. Her long bedazzled nails wrapped around her fork as she stuffed her favorite pancakes in her mouth to shut herself up before she said too much.

Trini had fallen hard to Riz and she wouldn't have things any other way. Aside from being caring and loving to her, he kept her laced in the latest fly shit from bags to shoes to bundles and nails. He introduced her shit that she had never even thought of before like having her eyebrows micro bladed and getting lash extensions done by Tali Michelle instead of gluing on her falsies daily. It was convenient and made her look flawless even without a bit of makeup.

"Lord, Zim is married and Trini is three seconds from being in love. What am I doing wrong?" Ivy joked once the waitress had come back to take her late order.

"All you have to do is start giving out chances. You're not going to find love by walking around with a stick up your ass."

"I don't." Ivy defended before trapping herself in her thoughts. Her comment was only a joke, but maybe Ivy knew was the reason that she was single.

She never minded being single or felt pressured to be in a relationship, but with the two ladies closest to her having the extra source of happiness, she couldn't deny that she might enjoy it. She would love to have someone to share events of her day with or cuddle while watching movies. And sex. Definitely sex, because while her toys always sufficed, there was nothing like some real dick with real rhythm and movements. And of course, real feelings attached. Quickly blinking the thoughts away, she sipped from her glass of water and scooped a forkful of eggs into her mouth.

"Well, I see what's new with Trini already." She chuckled. "Zim how are you? How's Marcus?"

"Girl, we keep getting into it about a baby. He wants me to get pregnant so bad and-"

"Well he is your husband. That's usually what you do when you're married." Trinity chimed in. While the three of them were close, she was still her best friend's younger sister so she didn't know everything about Zimora or her relationship.

"Marriage does not mean one person gets to make demands for the other. We discussed it before we got married and of course I was for it, but there are just changes that need to be made in our marriage before I can think about getting pregnant." Zim informed although she really wanted to say *"bitch, mind your business. You're nowhere near married. You don't understand."*

"Do you think maybe you two should go to therapy? Maybe a professional can vocalize everything that he doesn't seem to understand coming from you, "Ivy suggested, but neither Zimora or Marcus' pride would allow it.

"Maybe." She said simply, deading the conversation.

Comfortable silence washed over them as they finished their food in silence, enjoying one another's company. But the slurping sounds coming from Trinity's straw broke it. Taking the final sip of her orange juice and adjusting her bag on her shoulder simultaneously, she stood. "Her man must have said it's time to go, Zim." Ivy laughed and Trinity rolled her eyes, not amused.

"Fuck you." Trinity spat. She was slightly annoyed by the comment, even if it was the truth. "I love y'all." She assured before sliding a fifty-dollar bill down on the table to cover all of their meals and left out of the small breakfast restaurant and walked to the corner where Risen was parked.

"I still can't meet your sisters, huh?" Riz asked once Zim got into the passenger seat of his car. "For somebody who claims to not be embarrassed by me you sure do hide me a lot. Just like I can't meet your parents or your friends." He chuckled but she knew that he didn't find it funny. Risen didn't know much about relationships. He had only officially been with one other woman who proved to only want him because he had money. But he did know that he didn't like feeling played and that was exactly how Trinity had him feeling.

"Baby you know that's not it. I would love for you to meet my family but they won't be as accepting of you as I am. They'll judge you and I don't want that."

"I'm a grown ass man. I've been judged my whole life. But I'm just going to drop it. For someone who's so certain that they don't care about what other people think you sure seem to. But whatever."

Trinity grew saddened. She didn't want her man to feel like she was hiding him because it wasn't her intention. She would love to show her man off and invite him to dinners, but she would hate for her family to rip him apart. He could handle it, but she knew that no matter how hard he was it would hurt him.

"We have a long time ahead of us. We'll get there. Don't think I'm doing anything to purposely make you feel like I'm not all in because I am. I haven't met any of your family either, remember?" she asked before wanting to jump out of the moving vehicle once reality hit her.

"I don't have any fucking family, remember?" he mocked. Apart of her wanted to just take him inside of the restaurant and let him at least meet her sister, but he drove off quickly mumbling a halfway audible "Don't worry about it."

Zim and Ivy sat across from one another and Ivy noticed just how drained her best friend looked. "What's really going on?" She wondered and Zimora smiled.

"How do you know me so well?"

Ivy took a sip of her water and sat back, waiting for her friend to spill the beans on what had her visibly stressed.

"Maybe Trini's right. He is my husband, I'm supposed to, but I can't. And since he knows I don't want to, it's putting a damper on my marriage. Am I being selfish? Am I putting all of this on myself?" She wondered. Finally, she had aired it all out. The tears began to fall from her hazel eyes almost immediately. Taking the seat beside her, Ivy pulled her best friend into a side hug and rubbed her back. She couldn't comment on the situation because she never wanted to get into a married couple's business, but she provided a shoulder for her friend to cry on. Literally.

The waiter pretended not to see them as they sat there for another five minutes before pulling apart. Zimora began to pack up her bag and dap at her wet eyes.

"And I think he's cheating on me."

TWELVE

• • •

Koko carried a plate of mussels, shrimp, broccoli and French fries to the far left of the bar and sat it in front of Cassim's designated seat. "Thank you, sweetheart." He said, placing a one hundred dollar bill tip in her hand. She held onto his hand a little longer, trying to keep him from giving it to her. "That's a lot ." she laughed slightly. "You don't have to give me so much money."

"You're thinking too hard, ma. This is your job. Tips come with the territory. You do a good job, you deserve good tips." Dakota smiled and stuffed the bill into the fanny pack she sported. The bar wasn't busy at all since it was a rainy Tuesday evening.

Cassim grabbed his bottle of water off of the counter before turning slightly to look at Dakota. "Sit down and talk to me for a minute."

"I shouldn't. I don't want to be caught slipping on the clock. Plus I don't want to interrupt you while you eat." Cassim looked around the slightly empty bar and smiled. "I think you're good. If anyone needs your services I'll let you go."

Satisfied with his comprise, Dakota sat beside him hesitantly. "You sure you aren't a stalker? You're always in here but never drink."

He chuckled, almost spitting out his water and Koko smiled small.

"No man, I'm not a stalker. Stop insulting me. You don't like seeing me in here?" he wondered and watched her cheeks turn a hue of pink that not even the finest brand of blush could recreate. She didn't respond leaving the conversation opened for Cassim to gear it in any direction he wanted. So he did.

"You never called me," he said taking a sip from his water bottle.

Koko grew nervous, not expecting the conversation to go that way. But she should've expected it. They saw one another a lot and spoke like friends every time. It had been almost two weeks since he had given her his phone number and she had been debating with herself since the first night to call. She wasn't sure what it was about him that took her back to the days of having a middle school crush. But she felt stupid for being so giddy and wanted to wait until the feeling went away before finally calling. "I'm sorry. I really have been busy."

"I get that." He nodded. "I'm busy too. But I called you last night." He finally looked over at her, watching the overhead light dance on her skin. She didn't sport the full face of make up like before, she was back to modeling her nineties like subtle beauty with only a bit of lip gloss adorning her lips.

Koko picked her brain until she remembered seeing the call once getting out of the shower and being unsure whether or not she should call back.

"I'm sorry." She said simply, not even bothering with excuses. "I wasn't ignoring you or avoiding you. I just have to admit that you make me a little nervous."

His laughter was infectious and made her smile herself before he stared at her with squinted eyes. "Why would you be nervous around me? I'm nobody to be nervous around." He had to admit that he honesty drew him to her like a moth to a flame. He didn't know too much about her personality besides the fact that she was observant, polite, and feisty. The more he found out about her, the more captivated he became. She shyly shrugged. He could say that he was no one to be nervous around, but her mind didn't seem to understand that.

She had never met anyone who was as smooth and unreadable as Cassim Evans. His face was emotionless most times, until he smiled his bright white smile. She wasn't sure what to truly believe with him, so she tried to keep him at a distance. But he wouldn't allow it. And truthfully, she didn't really want to.

"All of that attitude you had when we first met and you want to be nervous." He laughed and she playfully hit his arm.

"That was a bad day. Shut up."

"Yeah? Then what made it turn into a good day? Because you ended it asking questions about me." He wondered as he adjusted himself in the seat and discreetly looked around the bar. People watching was one of his strongest suits.

"You smelled really good. And I didn't realize at first that you looked better." She felt comfortable enough to admit and watched him smirk slightly before taking another swig from his bottle.

"Well thank you."

A small comfortable silence washed over them as Koko too looked around the establishment to make sure that she wasn't needed. There was still only a handful of customers and she had to admit, she was enjoying how she was getting to spend her work day.

"So really, why are you always here if it's not to see me?" she wondered and looked up at him hoping to see a small smile that she was beginning to love.

"Who said it's not to see you?" He asked and couldn't even contain his laughter and the *nigga please* look she gave him. "No, but this is my mom's bar. I come to check on things from time to time. And she leaves me food." He told her and grew grateful that Akira's presence could be felt nearing them. He liked Dakota, but he was iffy about sharing his personal business with people. It gave him anxiety because he never knew who was preying on his downfall, but Koko was a girl that he was actually into so for her, he'd put it aside a little.

Kira noticed the two sitting close, laughing and talking and she couldn't help the smile that pulled at the corners of her mouth. "Well look at you guys." She hummed before leaning into Cash and whispering in his ear "Caine's in the back." Dakota quickly stood, feeling slightly guilty that she was on the clock but not working. Especially in the presence of her manager, even if it was her friend. "I have to go make sure the bar is stocked for tonight." She said as she went to walk away only for Cassim to grab her arm gently, not seeming to care that Akira was standing there.

"Answer when I call you." He said into her ear as he pulled her into a small hug. She smelled the familiar heavenly scent that she had the night at the restaurant and she almost melted into him.

She nodded in assurance as she looked up at him briefly before diverting her attention elsewhere. "Okay"

She walked off quickly and Cash eyed his surroundings before heading out back where Akira had already seemed to migrate to. He noticed her and his twin hugged up in a corner of the storage space where they conducted business. His hands were glued to her ass and her lips to his. Surprisingly, it wasn't disturbing even though he didn't want to see it. He was happy for his brother and Akira, who was like a sister to him anyway. Clearing his throat, he made his presence known and Kira pulled away from Caine.

"My dad is sending us some new shit at the end of the week." She began, but by the pause that followed, both brothers knew that there was more to come. "But he's coming this time."

"For what? He only comes if something is important." She was silent and Cash chuckled. "You have to meet your soon to be father in law."

Caine eyed Akira with a raised brow and when she didn't deny it, he huffed. "You told him already?"

"I mean was it a secret? Shouldn't I be proud of who my man is and brag about him?" her attitude was what turned Caine on, but also what turned him off at times.

"Come on with the attitude Kira I just asked a question."

"You know what. Don't even worry about it." She mumbled before going back up to the bar allowing the large space to be occupied by just Cassim and Cairo.

Caine left out and Cash traveled close behind. "Ride with me real quick." He requested and Cash hopped into the passenger seat of his car.

"Trouble in paradise already?" Cash asked, not being able to help himself with the jokes of his brother's love life.

"Fuck you. She's just dramatic as hell and she tells her dad everything. I'm too low key for that and I don't need my business mixed with my pleasure. Even if I am fucking his daughter." He laughed a little. "What's going on with you and the jawn from the bar though?"

Cash tucked his lip between his teeth and shook his head. "Nothing. We just see each other in passing and talk here and there now that she works at Chinx. I mean she's cute and shit, but we're just cool. She's cool."

"Yeah? That's why you have her calling you Cassim? Cause she's cool?" Caine smirked and looked over at his younger brother briefly before focusing back on the road.

"Everybody doesn't need to know Cash." He told him simply. To purposely draw attention to that side of him would be stupid. Especially to someone who didn't even seem to give a fuck that he had money. She didn't even know she was working at the bar that he owned.

Caine nodded, unable to argue with the logic. "Just be careful about getting involved with people outside of us. We already have cops lurking around in our shit. Plus, you've been hanging around the bar a lot more lately. You don't want to slip up chasing pussy bro."

Cash grew annoyed. "Don't ever disrespect me like that. I don't slip up and I damn sure don't chase pussy." He reminded. "And was all in your business when you were fucking any and everybody that your name could get you?"

"No, because I'd fuck them and never see or hear from them again. You're out here trying to build connections. Did you even fuck her yet?" He asked and Cash's silence let him know that they hadn't.

"Listen, I stay out of your business with Akira so you need to worry about what you need to be worried about."

"Akira is with us. She knows us. She's not a liability. I just don't want to see you lose focus."

It was amazing to Cassim how his brother noticed his interest in a woman and his first thought was to be concerned about business as opposed to his brother's happiness. "Just be careful. These bitches are for everybody. Make sure you're using your head and thinking with the right one." Caine finished as they pulled up to his house and Cash would honestly rather be at his own home. Risen's car pulled up behind Caine's then soon Akira's.

"Wasn't Reese and them supposed to be at this meeting too?" Cash asked, seeing that if they were, they were late and he was keen on punctuality.

"Naw I'll give them the rundown tomorrow or something. I don't want them at my house." Caine told him before they all sat around in his living room.

Reese, Harlem, Shizz, Nasir, and Ricky were the ones who got their products off of their hands to be distributed out. Nine times out of ten, it was probably one of their stupid ass corner boys that had either been running their mouth or doing too much to have officers at their place of business.

"So what should we do? Who has to go?" Riz wondered, his trigger finger itching at the thought.

"Nothing we can do right now but pay attention. Riz, you're trying to kill people like that wouldn't make shit worse for us. We need to stay out of the bar for now. Nobody is to go there but Akira until we feel it's time to." Cash said and everyone nodded in agreement.

"We can meet at the restaurant until-"

"No. No, we'll figure out a new location." Caine said as he paced slightly, stress washing over his face.

Akira stood and walked over to him, stroking the side of his face with her thumb. "Relax babe. Don't stress yourself out. Who knows, they may not have even been there for us. Maybe it was for Aleemah the bartender." She joked slightly and lightened the mood. Maybe Caine was right. Maybe Cash did need to find someone who knew this side of him. Maybe he did need someone who could understand that some days were more stressful than others and the reasons why. Maybe he couldn't get that from someone who only knew Cassim.

THIRTEEN

. . .

The mandarin cranberry candles that sat on the marble coffee table allowed a heavenly scent to linger about as well as set a calming mood for Koko. The television in front of her was stuck on food network and muted as she opted to enjoy the book in front of her instead. Kayla Andre's The Other Side of The Pastor's Bed was getting good and she was finding it hard to put the book down. Yet still, her mind forced her to put it on hold as thoughts of Cassim flooded in. She smiled to herself and stretched out on the plush couch.

When she met Cassim a little over a month prior, his presence annoyed her. Simply because she assumed he was like every other guy she had come in contact with. Now though, he stayed on her mind and she realized that he was anything but the guys she usually encountered. She actually had no idea what kind of guy he was because he was so mysterious. He didn't have any social media profiles, so she couldn't go lurking or looking at his pictures when she felt like it. She only saw him on the days he popped up at the bar. She didn't even see him at the restaurant when she chilled there with Kira. If she didn't see him at her job, she'd assume that she created his fictitious persona in her own head. But a being as beautiful as him with his dark skin and defined features could only be created by God himself.

With thoughts of him clouding her mind, she absentmindedly unlocked her phone and scrolled to his contact information. She stared at it for a few seconds, contemplating whether or not to hit the call button. They had spoken over the phone a few times, but each time she felt the same flutter in her belly. She was sure that it would be in overdrive since she was usually the recipient of the calls instead of the caller. Her breathing increased as the phone rang in her ear a few times and each time, her heart beat heavier.

"Hello?" he answered, his voice sounding a lot deeper over the phone. Her slow response made him greet her once more before she finally spoke.

"Hey. It's Koko," She responded, hearing loud noise in his background.

"I know," he chuckled before the noise silenced signaling that he had changed his location.

"Were you busy?" She wondered, stalling until her nerves settled.

"Not too busy for you,"

"Corny," she snickered, finally finding her place of comfort—losing the nerves that made her feel like child.

She stood from her place on the couch and paced around the small living room, unable to sit still as they spoke.

"What's up though? You were just thinking about me?" Koko could hear the smirk in his voice but still smiled.

"A little bit." She admitted, biting on the corner of her lip.

"Oh really?"

"Just a little." She told him, pinching her pointer finger and thumb together like he could see it. He chuckled though and shifting could be heard through the receiver.

"I'll take that."

"You should come over." She found herself blurting out and wanting to slap herself afterwards. "Whenever you have time." She finished softly.

He was quiet for a few seconds too long and Koko took those seconds to think of all the reasons why she shouldn't have said that to him. But when he responded with, *"Send me your address"* She was happy that she did.

Koko wasn't exactly sure when he would be there, but she jumped up and sprinted to the bathroom. She had to shower and clean up and pretend like she wasn't doing anything once he got there so she had to be quick. And she was. She had washed twice thoroughly and got out in eight minutes according to the time on the cell phone she checked every chance she could just in case he called.

She ran around the house with her toothbrush hanging out of her mouth like a chicken with its head cut off as she picked things up and put them in their rightful places. Taking a glance down at her phone, she saw that she had missed a text from Cassim pledging to be on his way twenty minutes prior. If she were in a cartoon it would definitely be that moment when fire blows out her ears. She was nervous for sure.

She rubbed lotion over her body and dressed for the night in burgundy satin pajama shorts paired with a black tank top. She sighed in relief when she saw that she was finished and he still wasn't there. She still had time to gather everything from her bed and neatly toss it into her nightstand drawer before hearing a faint knock on the front door. Following the noise, she placed a hand on the knob to give herself a quick pep talk in her head.

"Who is it?"

"Cassim." He said. She could feel how close he was before she opened the door instantly smelling that same enticing smell from the night they had met.

Like second nature she walked toward him as he outstretched his arms for a hug before leading him inside.

"Sorry it's a little messy. I've just been lounging all night" She apologized as she led him to the couch. "Did you eat? Are you thirsty?" She asked and he smirked, realizing that she was trying to avoid sitting beside him on the couch. She walked toward the kitchen and Cassim gently grabbed her arm, pulling her back. "Why are you so jittery? Didn't I tell you that you didn't need to be nervous around me?" He questioned, looking down at her staring intently.

"Yeah. I'm not nervous. I'm just-"

"You just," He mocked. "Sit down and talk to me."

Cassim pulled her down beside him onto the cream, plush love seat and looked around discreetly. Koko's apartment was small, but cozy and clean. Her one love seat made the living room seem bigger than it was. "You were just in here vibing, huh?" he asked, taking notice of her muted TV, lit candles and book that sat opened and faced down on the table.

"Yeah. I don't really do too much but sit in the house, read and watch the cooking channel" she snickered. "I'm a little boring." She admitted but Cassim was intrigued by her revelation. He didn't meet too many homebodies like himself, and it didn't make her boring at all in his mind.

"That's not boring. I'm the same way. I like movies though."

Koko looked up at him unsure of whether or not to believe him. He didn't look like the type to prefer being home. He looked like the complete opposite but she took his word for it. She eyed his appearance, and noticed he wore crisp white tee shirts often and his sneakers never held a scuff like they were fresh out of the box daily. The waves in his hair were mesmerizing. They were almost as mesmerizing as his perfect, smooth, blemish free chocolate skin. She watched his lips move as he asked her how her day was.

"It was good. I finally had a day to myself so I've been home relaxing. I've had a lot on my plate lately, but hey. What can I say? I wanted to eat right?"

"Right." Cassim chuckled at her analogy.

"How was your day? You look tired. I didn't mean to catch you at a bad time. I-"

"This is actually the most relaxed I've been in a couple of days. I'm always on the move it seems like." He told her honestly.

"You need to make some time for rest and relaxation. You can't focus completely on a task if you're drained. You have to take care of yourself."

Cassim didn't respond, only looked up at Koko. The concern on her face was adorable. He laughed slightly at the fact that she cared enough to be concerned.

"Look at you sounding like my mother or something." He joked, causing her to blush a little. "I like seeing you in this element. I see you finally took the stick out of your ass."

She bit her lip a little and looked up at him, avoiding his dark eyes. His presence—his **being**, rather, had her ready to risk it all. There was no denying the attraction between them, but she couldn't help but wonder if it was only physical for him. She

didn't want to be in another situation ship.

"What's on your mind?" he asked, reading her like a

book.

"I just um," She giggled before pausing, "I just wasn't

sure what we were doing here. I mean, I don't care I just like

clarity. And-" she continued, beginning to ramble as her nerves

got the best of her.

"I like you, Dakota." He assured and Koko released a

breath. "But what we do here depends on you. Are you done

giving me a hard time?" he wondered, brushing a stray piece of

hair behind her ear.

Her heart skipped and she nodded as a comfortable

silence wrapped around them before gravity pulled them closer

to one another. She didn't have time to think before his lips

magnetically connected with hers. They were soft and his

kisses sweet, but as one peck turned into two and two into

three, she realized he had a lot more to offer than soft lips. The

air around them grew steamy as he parted her lips with his

tongue. She placed her hands to his cheeks as an excuse to be even closer to him and bring him closer when she felt like he would pull apart. It was a moment she probably would never want to end.

She didn't realize just how strong his arms were until he draped one around her waist and pulled her into his lap with ease, allowing her to feel him harden between her legs. The small moan that escaped through her lips was an indicator for her that she was about to be a hoe. She hadn't had sex in a year but was ready to give it up to Cassim in all of twenty minutes.

"Wait," She said placing both hands against his chest and grew surprised that he stopped abruptly and stared at her attentively, giving her the floor to voice her concerns. She couldn't seem to find them though, so she simply stared back as she tried to control her breathing. Her eyes danced around his face trying to find an expression of ill intention that he didn't possess. She only saw lust filled eyes that made her panties wet. As she reminded herself that this was their first time chilling together and that he didn't want to seem easy, the devil on her shoulder reminded her that their connection was strong. They were grown enough to act on sexual tension and still like each other the next day. *Devil wins.* She thought to herself as she leaned back in, picking up where they had left off.

Instantly she became a dog in heat as she moved her kisses from his lips to his neck, feeling his grip on her waist tighten as she neared his ear. She etched a permanent note in her brain about the spot that seemed to be his favorite. The silence in the room made his heavy breathing and her small whimpers sound as loud as Mack trucks but neither of them seemed to mind. No longer able to help herself, Koko tugged on the hem of Cassim's shirt and lifted it up, praying that he didn't have a shirt underneath, but he did. She was a patient person, but it wasn't one of her best qualities when she was horny.

Cassim noticed her small pout and smirked before helping her out and removing his undershirt for him. He didn't have abs, but his chest and stomach were just as toned as his arms, even with his small pudge. She thought that she loved a man with tattoos, but seeing his canvas as clean as the day he was created was even sexier.

"Your turn," he told her as he lifted her own tank top over her head, letting her C cup breast free, surprised that shy Dakota didn't mind baring it all for him. If Koko was a dog in heat, he was a hungry one.

Did she think she'd ever be sharing such an intimate moment with him? Hell no. But was she going to take advantage of it and enjoy? Hell yes. She shifted her gaze toward her bedroom door and wondered if she could go from the couch to her bed without ruining the moment. Cassim, seeming to be a step ahead, scooped her up and made his way to her bedroom with her in his arms. The second she sunk it the memory foam mattress, Cassim was on top of her with his lips connected with her neck like a leech. Her reaction wasn't as subtle as his, as she hummed in satisfaction.

The more he stared at her with hooded eyes like he wanted to devour her, the more she anticipated how good he would feel inside of her. Finally, like he had been reading her mind, he reached between them and caressed her middle outside of the shorts she wore. He could feel the warmth and moisture from the outside and could only imagine how the inside would feel. He caught her by surprise when he slid the crotch area to the side and slid his finger inside of her, but he was too close to help himself.

"Don't tease me." She practically begged and the smirk that his mouth formed let her know that he was planning to fuck with her.

"Don't tease you?" He repeated, curving his fingers and pushing them in and out of her while flicking his tongue over one of her exposed nipples. "What should I be doing then?"

Koko's moans kept her from speaking which forced him to answer his own question. He slid down, taking her shorts and panties with him and buried his head between her thighs.

She stared down at him, her mouth agape as he slid his tongue in and out of her opening and over clit with a gentle roughness. She couldn't pry her eyes away, and his eyes being locked on hers didn't make things any better. She thought about all of the tricks she was going to pull out for him that she hadn't used in so long once she felt her legs begin to shake. Tossing her head back on the pillow, she cursed herself for looking away first and missing how sexy he had to look slurping up all of the juices she had just released.

"Don't get comfortable." He murmured, kissing her deeply as he removed his pants and boxers, the only articles of clothing keeping him from being as nude as Koko.

His dick fit him perfectly. Long, dark and veiny to his tall, dark, and handsome. It had the perfect length to width ratio in her mind, and she bit her lip knowing she could take it.

"Lay back." Koko demanded before he got the chance to lie on top of her. It had been a long time since she had been penetrated, but in her mind she was wet enough for him to slide right in.

"I look like I take orders?" He asked and Koko squinted her eyes at him as she moved herself closer to him.

"I look like I was taking no for an answer?" she rebutted, lying him back herself while climbing on top.

Gently sliding her fingertips over him, she grabbed ahold of his condom clad member and sat it at her entrance, smirking at how the heat of her middle made his dick tremble. Slowly, she slid down onto him and shut her eyes, taking it in gut wrenching pleasurable feeling. Watching him bite his lip and grip her waist like he was feeling the same.

Cassim and Dakota's hot and sweaty skin rubbed against one another's as they fought for dominance in a fit of passion. She was trying to keep her moans cute, but the way he pounded into her even from underneath had her screaming to the ceiling. And he was enjoying it for sure. He gripped her waist tighter and bit his lip harder while she rode him vigorously. Every curse word that passed his lips fueled her fire. She thought she was winning, but when he flipped her over and gave her long, deep strokes she knew it was only a game of losers. With one fist planted in the cushion of the bed, and the other hand on her chin to bring her lips to his, he fucked her until she screamed and moaned into his mouth.

"Wait." She whimpered, trying to hold onto her release. She wasn't ready for the moment to end. But just like her, he couldn't fight his much longer either.

They lied together silently in the disheveled sheets after their climax. There was no way that after the hour that had just passed they could go back to tell-tell glances at the bar. Koko knew that one night with Cassim just wouldn't be enough for her. And by his light snoring as his head rested on her chest, she knew that it wouldn't be.

FOURTEEN

• • •

Ivyana let the cool morning breeze fully wake her as she sat in front of her building on a nearby bench. She was dressed in denim booty shorts, a cropped tank top and a large satin scarf on her head. It wasn't a look she would ever go out of the house in, usually. She was on a mission though.

It was only just before seven in the morning and it was quiet since kids were no longer in school. Kids in the morning were rowdy so it was refreshing to have early morning peace. She was feeling sluggish herself though. She had been waiting for the young corner boy who was playing the block to come out for about twenty minutes. If he were good, his ass would definitely be up and at them. If he was great, he might have been out all night and still at it. Being a drug dealer was just too time consuming to Ivy. Why would anyone ever want to lose sleep and risk their lives all at once? Then she remembered that her job description wasn't too different.

Soon enough, before the clock struck seven his Adidas slides were hitting the concrete. He wore basketball shorts, and a tank top since it was said to be a high of eight-nine degrees. Just by sizing him up Ivy knew that talking to him should be a breeze. She stood and placed her phone to her ear, talking loudly before walking into his view. As expected, he did a double take giving her the opportunity to catch his attention.

"Hold on, girl." She said to the imaginary caller before staring up at the guy. "Where Reese at?"

She knew that the bold sentence would either get her good information or no information, but it was the only way that she could think of so it was a risk she had to take. He stared at her for a while like a deer caught in headlights.

"Hello?" Ivy snapped slightly, snapping her fingers. "If you don't know just give me his number real quick. I have to go, but I need to talk to him. He knows me. I'm Paige." Ivy rolled her eyes, hoping that he felt bad for not remembering her. But he didn't. Poor thing seemed confused.

"Who's Reese?" he asked, like he was coached. Ivy was surprised. When she first saw him he was running his mouth for no reason, now he was lying. *Somebody fucking got to him before I could.* She thought to herself and wondered who it was, how and why.

As far as she knew, she was the only officer on their case from that angle. But if he was as reckless as he seemed, Ivy probably wasn't the only one who had overheard one of his boasting conversations. It was probably Reese who had told the young boy to watch the shit that came out of his mouth. Or maybe the order came from higher up. Like Cash and Caine who she had yet to get to. Her plan was backfiring and after three months, she thought maybe she was beating a dead horse.

"Don't worry about it." Ivy huffed before hanging up the phone and sticking it in the back pocket of her shorts as she walked away.

The sounds of cars speeding by in the early morning traffic were almost therapeutic to Ivy as she continued her walk deep in thought.

"Or maybe he fucking knew you were a cop, dummy."

She mumbled to herself. Maybe it was true what she heard.

That it was easy to spot and undercover cop. For all she knew,

they could've already been on to her and she'd be dead by the

morning.

"I'm really not cut out for this," she whispered to

herself before pulling off.

Self-doubt was something that Ivy never thought much

about. She tackled everything head on and didn't take no for an

answer, but she was starting to think that maybe she wasn't the

person for the job. Maybe there actually was someone better

than her that could get farther than her. These twins were too

smart.

It was like a ghost town in her neighborhood but that

was probably because all of the action started after noon. Once

back inside her home, she snatched her clothes off and

wrapped herself in a towel, but before she could shower she

needed to make a call.

Jonathan Gates answered on the third ring and Ivy didn't even exchange greetings before beginning her rant. "John, you really have to give me something else to work with. I'm drawing blanks all across the board. I'm doing my job. I am. I'm asking around, I'm people watching, I'm scoping the neighborhoods, I'm asking the junkies. I've even asked the loud mouth school kids. And you know they know something. They always know, but even they aren't saying anything." She said all in one breath as she paced. She was starting to feel the pressure from the case. She couldn't be around her family, around her friends and on top of that, she was failing.

Papers could be heard shuffling in the background and she sighed in relief, hoping that he would come up with something that could help her. "We really don't have a lot of information, Ivy. I can't do anything about that-"

"Well if we don't have that much information, why the hell are we even on the mission so soon?" she semi-snapped, cutting him off. For a second, she had forgotten that this was

Detective Gates she was speaking with. "Sorry. I'm just. It's just frustrating." She admitted on the verge of tears.

"And that's what makes you a good officer. I know it's a lot of pressure, and I get that. I understand your frustration and I'm on your side. Every bit of information I get, I share with you." He told her. But it still didn't explain to Ivy why they were building a case on people they didn't have much information on.

The shuffling of his pages ceased, leaving them both silent since Ivy didn't bother to respond. "Their nicknames are Cash and Caine, but one of them is named Cairo I hear. No last name as of yet. They've had ties to a location on Front and Girard. They were also said to have been spotted near or around a bar by the name of *Chinx*. But that's not verified yet. We're all working very hard."

"Wait a minute. How could they have been spotted or said to be anywhere when I haven't reported anything?" Ivy questioned only for Detective Gates to grow silent. "Right, so now I can't do my job." She chuckled in annoyance.

"Don't think of it like that, Officer Atkins. I just know how hard it has been for you. It doesn't hurt to have help sometimes. I really want to catch these bastards. Sooner than later." He tried to reason, but Ivy hung up and tossed her phone in a fit of rage.

"Fuck this shit." She mumbled under her breath, although she headed right back out in preparation to work even harder.

She found herself driving around in circles with no destination until she made it to her best friend's house. She hadn't even planned on showing up. She hadn't called or texted, so she wasn't even sure if Zimora was home. But still she hopped out and walked up her front steps anyway. It was a Sunday, so luckily for Ivy Zimora was home, blasting gospel music and cleaning her spacious home.

She had been feeling like a horrible friend lately. To both Zimora and her younger sister. She hadn't been able to chill with them like she wanted to and even though they were understanding, it was taking a toll on her. "Look at you, bitch!"

Zimora cooed. She was putting up a front. She was just as drained as Ivy was. She could tell from the bags under her eyes.

"Hey! I missed you. I had to pop up one time." Ivy lied, smiling small as she followed Zim inside.

"You're a bad liar." Zimora chuckled as Ivy found her way to the kitchen.

"So are you." She reminded as she pulled the opened bottle of wine from the fridge. "Grab the glasses."

The gospel music that played had turned into nineties rhythm and blues as the two best friends sipped on sweet red wine and ate crackers, cheese, and grapes like the stuck up, boujie bitches they slightly were. "So you're telling me he actually is cheating?" Ivy wondered with wide eyes. Zimora nodded and finished her glass before pouring another. "It's like," She began with slurred words. "It's like, you can walk around the house and not speak to me some days, have anger issues, put your hands on me, kick me when I'm down and still have the nerve to cheat on me?" she chuckled bitterly.

158

"The girl is beautiful though." She mumbled and Ivy tossed the rest of her own glass back.

"Wait, you've seen her?"

"Yeah, I went through his phone while he was sleeping. Stupid ass fell asleep with it unlocked. "He has a whole family." Zimora said, no longer able to mask her tears as laughter. "Some light skinned bitch named Chyna. They're engaged, with a three-year old daughter. And a son on the way. How can you commit to marry a woman when you already have a wife?" she cried and Ivy instantly stood to wrap her arms around her friend.

Her breakdown was necessary, but it still hurt Ivy to see her friend so broken. So hurt. "He doesn't deserve you, Zim. He never did. You can afford a nice condo on your own. I don't think he-"

"Just save the speech, Ivy." She mumbled. "We both know that I'm not really going anywhere.

Her revelation forced silence to flow through the roomy kitchen. But it wasn't Ivy's job to tell her friend what to do or judge the decision she made. It was her job to be there for her. So that's what she did.

Picking up her best friend's phone and eyeing the screenshots of her husband's fiancé and their family she smiled small. "Well, at least you know he only got with her because she looks like you."

FIFTEEN

. . .

Dakota yawned and slung her large tote bag over her shoulder as she finished her shift. She had slipped a pair of track pants over her body suit to walk out in. The guys gawked over bartenders and bottle girls just like they did over strippers and Koko didn't care for the attention. She just wanted to leave and wash the day off of her and lie down. Her phone vibrated inside of her bosom just as she stepped out of the door and saw Cassim across the parking lot with his phone glued to his ear.

No matter how tired she was she couldn't hide the genuine smile she held when she saw him. He placed his phone into the pocket of his grey sweats. "Hi handsome." She greeted, pecking his lips but the small peck he placed to her lips wasn't like how they usually were.

"Everything okay?" She wondered, growing concerned.

"Yeah." He told her, opening the passenger door to his 2002 Pontiac Bonneville.

It was Cassim's first car and his first big purchase, so he would never get rid of it. He just wanted to see Koko's reaction to it as opposed to the 2017 Benz she didn't know he pushed. He liked Koko. And had been battling with himself on whether or not he would like her the same, more, or less when she found out that he might not be exactly who she presumed him to be. He was expecting for her to turn up her nose at his vehicle of choice, but she only tilted her head back against the headrest and sighed of exhaustion. "You had a long day?" He wondered and she only nodded, grabbing ahold to his free hand.

"Yeah, but how was your day? Why do you seem so distant?"

Koko had come a long way from being shy, giddy and nervous Cassim. Now, she loved to be all up under him. He could deny it, but he liked it too. It was nice having someone to end long days with, even though they weren't official. He would always find himself at her place even if it were just for her company. He knew that he had to figure out sooner than later if she was worth it, because he could feel their connection growing and he'd hate to have to end things with her. But he would if necessary.

"Just thinking about some shit." He told her as they came to a stoplight. He watched the hue of red dance across her face, forcing him to stare a little longer at her tired expression. "You got money on you?" he asked once the light turned green. He pulled onto a deserted street, with a Chinese store across from it.

"Only twenty dollars." She told him pulling it out of the fanny pack on her waist and handing it to him. "You need it?" He smirked and looked at her. "That's all you have?"

"Well, on me. I have money home, I-"

"And you're willing to give it to me?" He quizzed with a raised brow.

"I mean, I know you wouldn't ask me if you didn't need it. I'm okay with the money I have home. I don't really need anything right now." She giggled and Cassim smiled, taking the crumpled bill from her hand.

"Come on." He told her as he hopped out of the car.

Koko's mouth watered for a pizza roll and homemade iced tea, a Chinese store specialty, but to her surprise they didn't go inside of the store. They instead walked across the street where a red Mercedes sat that Cassim unlocked with the key fob. "Get in," he requested seeing how skeptical she was.

"Whose car is this?" she asked, although she watched him press the start button and peel off once she was inside. "Mine." He answered simply.

"So whose car were we just in?" She was too tired for how confused she was.

"Mine." He chuckled as he dug into the middle console and pulled out five one hundred dollar bills. Placing her twenty back on top, he handed the bills to her. "Thank you."

Dakota, now fully awake, sat up in her seat and inspected the six bills like they held diseases and looked at Cassim who only faced forward.

"What is going on?" she wondered, sitting up as straight as she could in her seat. "Cassim!" She almost yelled, realizing the few seconds he was silent was too long for her. She needed answers.

"I like you." He told her before pausing until he came to a vacant Rite Aid parking lot. It was well after midnight, so it wasn't too bad of a place to have the necessary conversation he was dreading having. "I like you, but you only know pieces of me. So before I get too involved or get you too involved, I wanted to see if you were rocking with me for real." He admitted and was taken aback by Koko's chuckles.

"Oh so you were testing me? You wanted to make sure I would accept you in your Bonneville before I got to ride in your Benz? You claim you like me but automatically thought the worst of me?" she wondered and he realized her chuckles were not those of amusement. "Fuck you." She huffed getting out the car.

Cassim huffed in frustration as he stepped out as well. He leaned against the hood of his car with his arms folded across his chest as he watched Koko walk across the parking lot.

"Dakota." He called in a soft, but stern voice. There weren't too many times he called her Dakota instead of Koko, but it didn't take her long to realize that was his serious tone. She turned to face him, but didn't bother walking forward.

"Come here when you're done having your moment so we can get in the car and talk. We're not about to cause a scene in public."

She wanted to stand across from him and pout, but she was curious. So she slowly stepped forward until she was in front of him. His headlights shined against the wall it was in front of as they stood between them.

No words were exchanged as they stared at one another. Cassim's lip tucked between his teeth and Koko's arms folded across her chest.

"If you're expecting me to apologize, I'm not." He started, and grabbed her hand before she could begin her rant. "I'm a business man, so I have to protect myself and my shit. I would expect you to do the same thing and I wouldn't be mad at you for it."

"So now you're trying to tell me how I'm supposed to feel too?"

"Listen, don't do that. Don't listen to what the fuck I'm saying and only hear what you want." He demanded. His voice was low, but firm and if Koko wasn't pissed off with him, she'd find it sexy. "If you fuck with me, you fuck with me. And if you don't, you don't. The decision is yours."

Cassim wasn't for confrontation that had no ending. He preferred to get to the point or leave it alone. Koko really liked Cassim, so she didn't want to let his money or lack thereof ruin the connection they had.

"Are you," she began, but wasn't sure if she really wanted to ask. She wasn't sure if she really wanted to know. Her hands grew clammy as she wiped them on her pants. "Are you a drug dealer?"

His roar of laughter subsided her uneasiness and she released a sigh. "A drug dealer?" he asked with mock offense. "No baby, I'm not a drug dealer."

SIXTEEN

. . .

The smell of fried chicken snuck through the crack of Risen's closed bedroom door, but his mind couldn't focus on the inviting scent. He paced back and forth between the four walls and huffed as he listened in on the conference call he was having with Cash and Caine. With the burner cell glued to his ear, he pulled his iPhone from his pocket and shot Trinity a text letting her know that he would join her in a second.

Riz had never seen his brothers, his mentors worried, but with police popping up at one of their most prominent places of business, they had to get in front of whatever was going on. "Out of nowhere though? Y'all haven't made any enemies lately have you? Y'all taking niggas' bitches or something? Because I don't understand." Riz huffed. In the event that something needed to be handled, he would be the one doing it and he had actually been keeping his word of laying low.

"Shut up." Caine semi-snapped. Which was a clear indicator of his stress.

Truthfully, they hadn't had any slip ups, but Risen's words made the wheels in Caine's head spin. It had to be from a source inside.

"Whatever happened to that greedy ass cop that used to work for us? You think he's just fucking with us? Obviously they have nothing if no moves have been made." Cash asked the questions that ran through his mind. Before he could respond, Risen's door busted opened and Trinity stood before him with a plate of fried chicken, corn and mashed potatoes.

She wasn't a chef, but she wanted to be able to cook for her man and know what she was doing. The meal was too simple to be something her mom would make, but Riz was appreciative of it. Still though, when she saw him standing before her with wide eyes and two phones she squinted her eyes at him.

"Who the fuck have you been on the phone with while I'm in there cooking for you and shit?" She snapped, making sure she was loud enough for whoever was on the phone to hear.

"Yo can you fucking chill?" he snapped back, embarrassed that the twins were chuckling in his ear. "You drawing."

Growing annoyed with their laughter, he hung up the burner cell and tossed it onto his dresser. He turned to face Trini, but she had already walked out of the room and by the way the plate she held slammed against the table he had to wonder if there would even be food on there by the time he made it to the dining area.

"Are you done acting like a fucking child? Throwing tantrums and shit?" He asked, his voice raising an octane. She didn't respond, only grabbed her bag, tucking her notebook and pens inside along with her phone and keys.

"Where are you going?" He huffed in irritation, but she ignored him until she made it to the door.

"Listen Risen. I don't like secrets and you're a real sneaky nigga. I don't have time to be investing my time into you, and growing to love you when you're lying to me."

"What the fuck do I need to lie to-" he began before pausing. He stared into her dark, skeptical orbs. "You love me?" he asked instead of responding and she huffed as she walked further toward the front door. Her kinky afro bounced as she walked hard with anger.

"I'm just going to leave. I can be lied to in the comfort of my own home." She mumbled and Riz quickly grabbed ahold of her waist and pecked her cheek from behind.

"I'm not lying to you." He whispered into her ear. "I'm not messing around on you. You're supposed to know that already. You don't trust me?"

"Don't try to flip this, Riz. Seriously." She whined slightly. "Don't tell me one thing then do some sketchy shit that I'm supposed to accept because I trust you."

"There's nothing to accept. I'm not lying to you. Don't I always keep shit one hundred with you? Why would I lie now?

171

And if I was messing around on you, would I be talking to a bitch with you in the next room?"

"Niggas are stupid." She reminded, not backing down causing Risen to chuckle.

He grabbed her hand pulling her back toward the couch and sat down, pulling her into his lap. She didn't put up much of a fight, so he knew that she was at least willing to hear him out. So he knew that he had to be honest. Riz grabbed her chin in his hands and pulled her face to his, placing a small peck on her lips although he was unsure of how accepting she would be.

"You asked me what I do to drive around in a Maserati at twenty and I kept it simple with you. I told you that I wasn't a good nigga, but told you I would be good to you and you never brought it up again because you knew I held true to my words. I've been good to you, right? And I'm not just talking about the money I give you, the clothes and shoes I buy you, the jewelry. But don't I devote all of my free time to you? So why would you doubt me? Because you're listening to your bitter ass friends and waiting for me to turn into the niggas that they deal with?" he wondered but her silence wasn't the answer he was looking for.

He was making every word that passed his lips sound good and Trinity began to question whether or not she was overreacting.

"I can't tell you everything, babe. And it's for your protection, but I'm not out here making you look goofy or anything. I promise." He told her, pecking her lips once more. But this time with a little more passion.

"Do I need to be worried about you?" Trini asked, finally finding her words.

"I'm good baby. I'm about to go to school like you. You got a nigga motivated and shit." He joked forcing small giggles to escape his girlfriend's mouth.

"I hate you."

"I love you too."

His words lingered in the back of her head as she smiled big. He loved her, and she would do whatever to make sure he knew she loved him too.

EIGHTEEN

. . .

"How are you going to plan a big breakfast and not help me with this shit?" Koko asked Akira who was trying to sneak off upstairs to shower. Koko had already made the homemade waffles, grits, eggs, turkey sausage, and home fries. "You could at least cut up the fruit or make the mimosas."

She was nervous as hell, which was partially the reason she had made the majority of the food herself. Akira had planned a big breakfast with the both of them and their men. Koko had never met Akira's boyfriend and she wondered how Cassim would interact with him, but since he was close with Akira if Koko was lucky, he knew him already.

"Gyal me know noting about breakfast food." She joked with a giggle. "I can only cook Jamaican food. My boyfriend actually cooks the majority of the time."

"Wait," Koko paused with realization. "Why am I even doing all of this? He's not my boyfriend. I don't-"

"Girl. You're thinking way too hard. All this time that's passed? That's your nigga." She chuckled as she ran up the stairs, leaving Koko to cut up fruit and make mimosas but she seemed to need to do something to pass the time anyway.

Although Dakota and Cassim had been seeing one another for five months and had spent the entire summer together, she still found her stomach tightening as she thought about what she would wear. And she still found that her heart sped up when his name popped up on her phone screen. Smiling to herself, she popped the strawberries, into a bowl then the same with the pineapples, bananas and watermelon.

Akira nervously paced her bathroom as she put on a slight coat of make-up. Koko was her friend, Caine was her man, and she had known Cash for years. But she knew that by all being in one room together, they would have a lot of explaining to do. Caine wasn't prepared to add anyone into their small circles, but with his brother and girlfriend both vouching for Dakota, he realized he could meet her for himself.

Then he'd be able to size her up rightfully and decide whether or not she would be good for business and for his brother.

Unbeknownst to Dakota, Cassim walked into Akira's home through the front door. She had left it unlocked knowing that he and his twin would be arriving at any moment. From the entrance, he could see Koko maneuvering around the opened kitchen with a spatula in hand and satin, baby pink shorts with a white tank top that could have passed for pajamas. He knew because he had seen her in satin pajamas on quite a few occasions. His initial thought was sliding them to the side and going to work on her lady parts, like he had the first time they had sex. Nobody knew exactly how much time Cash and Koko had been spending together, but they didn't need to know. Caine had already expressed his distrust for her and with Akira being his woman, neither of them needed to be in their business. Plus, it was sexier when she could look at him in a room with her friend and keep it short then ride his dick once they left. Akira didn't know that they had had sex or she would've realized that there was no way they'd still be in the distant admiration stage. One taste of the flesh and you're a goner.

Cash snuck up behind Koko and wrapped his arm around her waist, forcing her to jump and drop the fork that had replaced the spatula in the time he stood watching her. "What the fuck!" she exclaimed as she hit his chest and held her own simultaneously. She hadn't even had time to finger comb her hair knowing she still had yet to get dressed since Akira was still in the bathroom. "You scared me babe. You're early."

"Or am I right on time?" he shot back, pecking her lips and grabbing a sausage link off of the stove at the same time. He took a bite before Koko could pop his hand and he smiled. He pecked her cheek, to get an extra whiff of her natural fragrance before giving her a proper greeting. "Hey beautiful."

"Hey." She smirked, finally getting a good look at him. Summer had come and gone, leaving fall to bring forth great weather days and even better outfit days. Cassim was dressed in a white button up shirt with the sleeves rolled up, showcasing the Rolex watch he had gotten to match his twins', denim distressed jeans, and classic butter colored timberlands. His fresh hair cut was simply the icing on top. "You look nice." She observed as she cut off the stove and began to place the platters of food onto the dining room table buffet style.

"Where's Kira?" He asked, opening his mouth for the forkful of grits she was feeding him knowing that they were his favorite.

"She's upstairs getting dressed, like I don't have to get dressed too." She huffed, feeling sweaty from the heat of the kitchen although she had showered.

"Well since it's just you and me right now." He mumbled, pulling her into him and sending youthful giggles throughout the kitchen. He pecked her lips twice and stopped himself from going in for a third, knowing if he did he'd have her on top of Akira's counter top. "I wanted to talk to you about something."

"And what's that?" she hummed, wrapping her arms around his torso while being engulfed in the scent of Pi by Givenchy.

Koko chuckled on the inside at how his body stiffened slightly against her like he was nervous. "I mean, since we've been vibing real heavy lately, we might as well see where this takes us." He said and Koko realized just why he might be nervous.

"Where this takes us?" She questioned for clarity.

"Yeah, where this relationship takes us." He mumbled and watched her smile genuinely, allowing the gesture to reach her eyes.

"That was smooth, Cassim."

"Yeah? So that means you're mine or do I still have to share?" he joked while she flicked his side.

"You were never sharing." She winked and pulled back, but not before passionately kissing him as the answer he was looking for. He pulled away, hearing movement near the stairs and didn't want to hear Akira's mouth about what he and Koko were doing. She was like a child and would be cooing over it for the whole day.

"What's up with these girly ass drinks and shit? This is not brunch with your girlfriends." He wondered and roared in laughter at the side eye she had given him.

"I'm joking baby. You know I love your fake food networking cooking ass."

"Huh?" she asked, stopping in her tracks to look at him, while he looked at her as well like a deer caught in the headlights.

"Bro!" Kira yelled, making her presence know. Cash gave her a side hug while Koko still stood stuck in a trance trying to figure out if her mind was playing tricks on her or if Cassim had just told her that he loved her. "Where is your brother with his late ass?"

"Awe, you're dating his brother?" Koko asked, although slightly embarrassed that she didn't even know he had a brother. "How cute is this?" She gushed. "Let me go throw on my clothes real quick before he gets here." She announced while jogging up the steps.

Although she had showered already, she needed the quick five-minute shower that she had taken. She left her face make-up free and sighed as she stared at her reflection in the mirror for longer than expected. Hearing an extra voice downstairs, she slipped into her own distressed jeans and paired it simply with a tank top that would go under her cropped hoodie once she was prepared to leave.

Cassim's eyes found hers as she walked toward the table, since he was facing her way. His brother's back was to her and Akira leaned over him, whispering in his ear. "She's coming now baby. Be nice. Please." She mumbled and she suddenly felt nervous. He wasn't only her friend's boyfriend, he was her boyfriend's brother and she wanted to make sure he liked her. Kira planted a final kiss on his cheek and sat beside him as Koko walked into his view.

"Hi, nice to meet-" She began once he turned to face her and accept her greeting. But she instead turned to Cassim, wondering if she had mistakenly gone to greet her own man instead. "you." She finished, turning back to his brother. His twin brother.

"Nice to meet you too. The food looks good. I know Akira didn't cook all of this."

"Shut your stupid ass up." She snapped, slapping his head. "This is why we can't ever be cute. You always have to be stupid." She whined only causing him to laugh.

"I'm joking, relax. Damn."
But Dakota had tuned out their whole conversation.

Her skin had begun to heat up instantly and she rubbed her clammy hands down her jeans. Slowly, she walked toward Cassim and sat beside him.

"You okay, babe? You look like you've seen a ghost." He chuckled and she forced a smile before quietly sticking a strawberry in her mouth.

NINETEEN

. . .

Koko hadn't been herself for majority of the weekend
after the bomb dropping breakfast at Akira's. Cassim had been
blowing her phone up, probably regarding his slip up that
expressed his love. But Dakota was more concerned with all
the secrets of Cassim's life that were recently coming out. But
even with how much he was calling, and how tight her stomach
got when he did she still hadn't answered.

A heavy knock on her apartment door frightened her
slightly. It was one of the things she hated about living alone in
the neighborhood she lived in. Sitting silently on the sofa, she
looked at the time on the cable box and saw that it was well
after ten at night. "Oh hell no. That's not for me." She
mumbled, but the person knocking continued and her heart beat
against her chest. When they knocked the third time, she
slowly got up and walked to the door wishing that it had a
peephole. "Who is it?"

"Open the door, Dakota." Cash's voice sounded and she quickly pulled the door opened with her shaky hand. "You scared?" he wondered, noticing her alarming demeanor. She didn't respond, but he walked in and didn't hesitate to remind her "you would've known it was me had you been answering the fucking phone. Why you iggin' me?"

"Nobody's ignoring you Cassim." She lied while he read right through her.

She noticed that in his hands he held a bag from Kingston's Caribbean Cuisine, Akira's family restaurant.

"I brought food, so let's talk." He suggested, not seeming to give her much of an option. Truthfully, her ignoring him was bothering him. It was as if the very thing he didn't want to happen was happening. She was distancing herself from him.

"Why does it seem like you have so many secrets?" Koko asked him before he could even set their food trays in front of them. He ignored her until he was positioned on the floor beside her with his back against the sofa.

"Nothing I do is a secret. It's just not for everybody at every moment." He told her calmly.

"But me? We're together and I didn't even know you had a twin brother?"

"We literally just got together three days ago, Koko. I would be an idiot to expose every aspect of my life to a stranger. Yeah, we were vibing and yeah we were cool, but neither of us really knew that we would end up here and you know that. Plus, I'm sure there's a lot about you I don't know as well, so what's the real reason you're upset?"

Koko's words were trapped in her throat and she hadn't even touched the delicious smelling platter in front of her.

"Nobody knows I have a twin unless they know us personally. And if they know us personally then they know why no one knows that I have a twin." He told her, as if it was supposed to make sense just because it was said in his deep, raspy tone. He was tired. And as Koko paid more attention to him, he even looked tired. Drained, rather.

"You look tired, why don't you go lay down and we can finish this conversation in the morning?" Koko suggested, but that wasn't Cassim's plan.

"No I want to just get everything out and on the table so we can figure out where to go from here." He told her, showing her that it was really bothering him.

"Okay," she began, closing her food up and turning to her side to face him. "Let's talk. Everything you want me to know."

He eyed her with an elongated stare and thought about everything he was about to say before he said it. The only other time he had to have a conversation, it was with his parents and he was fortunate enough to be able to do it with Cairo. Now though, he was on his own and he couldn't even deny being nervous.

"Take your shirt off." He almost demanded, and Koko blinked rapidly, not recognizing the tone. "Let me make sure you aren't wearing a wire or some shit."

"Are you serious?" She chuckled, but he was definitely serious. "Why would I be wearing a wire?" she wondered as she quickly removed the t-shirt she wore that belonged to him. She did a spin, showing him her wire free bra and panties and he seemed to feel a little more comfortable.

"I'm not going to lie, the shit I'm about to tell you could really fuck me up if it were to be heard or repeated. I really don't-"

"Do you trust me?" Koko asked, stroking his cheek with her thumb. "Because you said you loved me, so isn't trust usually included in that?"

Her voice was gentle enough to rock a baby to sleep, but Cassim was still skeptical. He was putting his life and his livelihood at risk by even beginning to show Koko his other face. But he loved her. And he knew she loved him, but how could she if she didn't really know him fully? And although he was a grown ass man, he knew it really would crush him if he had to deal with his first time being in love. And his first heart break back to back if she decided she no longer wanted to be with him.

"Not everyone knows me as Cassim Evans." He began, his voice in a slight whisper. "Some know me simply as Cash. And those who don't know me as Cash know my brother, Cairo as Caine. You asked me before if I was a drug dealer, and I told you that I'm not. And I didn't lie." He promised. "I'm a drug distributor, my brother and I. Once our shipments come in, and we pass them off to the niggas with desires to sell that shit, our hands are wiped clean. Money up front. But because of our job description, Caine and I are hardly ever in public together. Only our family, the people who work with and for us know who we are. And we do things that way, because if we were to ever get picked up and a cop asks some shit like where is your twin, we know that the information came from inside of our circle."

Koko nodded, taking in the newfound information. Blinking rapidly, she continued to stare up at him, wondering how she had gone so long without realizing there was so little she knew about Cassim. His mysteriousness was one of the things that she was attracted to, but she didn't think he was this mysterious.

"I'm not ashamed by what I do, but I wanted to give you the option to decide for yourself whether that was something you could handle and deal with by being with me.

"I appreciate that." She told him before there was a slight pause.

Cassim stared at her, waiting for her eyes to show him any sign of skepticism. But the only thing they seemed to hold was nervousness. Testing his luck, he held out his hand for her to grab even though she was sitting right beside him. He pulled her across him and into his lap once her hand fell into his. Like second nature, she draped her arms around his neck while his found his way to her waist. Still though, they didn't say anything.

"What made you want to do this? Were you a corner boy or something and just wanted more" she finally asked. She wasn't judging, but she always wondered how someone would go about making the decision to risk peace of mind and death for a monetary goal.

"No, I've never sold drugs. I never wanted to sell drugs either, but nobody hustled harder than my pop when I was younger." He began. "Every hustle doesn't have to involve drugs or illegal shit. But since I always saw my dad making ways and finding ways to get money, I started to do the same. My brother and I both did. Caine used to buy all this candy from the papi store to sell in school and I used to make CD's of all the shit people wanted to hear and sell them in school. The mentality just stuck. But this shit kind of just fell in my lap. Came in contact with the right people, used my books smarts and here I am. I mean, I never thought this would be my money mission. But I'm definitely not mad that it is." He admitted and Koko was intrigued. She knew that he wasn't telling her everything and she couldn't wait to hear more of his stories. But as much as it intrigued her it also worried her.

He licked his bottom lip out of habit before chuckling as he realized that the look in her eyes was concern. "You

191

don't have to worry about me." He promised. "I'm good at what I do. And I'm not a dumb nigga. I actually have a bachelor's in criminal justice." He laughed. "Go figure. But when a year passed after my graduation and I still couldn't find a job, I made my own. And I can guarantee I make way more than I would even if I worked in my field." Koko noticed how with every word he spoke, the lighter his mood got and she could tell he didn't talk about it often. "I was going to be a youth probation officer, to help kids that were going downhill early. Kids like my youngboul Risen that works for us. I feel like shit most days knowing that he shouldn't be into this shit. He just turned twenty but I knew that if I didn't take him under my wing he'd be doing life right now. He was a sixteen-year old drop out with charges against him. His fate was already sealed for him. It's like a lose-lose situation with that one." He vented, letting out feelings he had never expressed before. His brother didn't always think like him, so he didn't really care. He was more of a *"why should I feel bad because this is what you want to do"* type of person so he wouldn't even understand. That's why Cash was happy to have Koko. To express things that she couldn't express to anyone else. It was crazy because usually he would be skeptical, but he trusted her. And for her to win his trust meant she had to be the one for him, because he didn't trust easily.

"Your intentions were good. You wanted to see him do better and he is, right? He isn't doing life." She told him, making him nod in agreement.

"I guess." He mumbled, and Koko knew that that was something that would fuck with him for a while.

Catching her off guard, he grabbed ahold of her chin and pulled her into him. He didn't kiss her immediately, only stared to see if she would be hesitant. But she wasn't. In fact, it was her who had crashed her lips into his. With her hand rested on his cheek, her eyes bored into his as they kissed passionately. Psychologists would say that people kiss with their eyes closed because having your eyes opened would be an overload on the brain and hinder pleasure, but as Koko and Cassim shared tale-tell glances they knew that couldn't be

193

anything further from the truth. In fact, nothing had ever felt so perfect.

Koko hadn't realized that she was shedding tears until Cassim had used his thumb to brush them away. "What you crying for?" he wondered and she chuckled.

"I don't know. I just. I don't really know what I'm getting myself into." She admitted

"I'm giving you an out if you want it." Cash reminded, but Koko knew that that was the last thing she wanted.

"I don't want an out."

"Good." He smirked, pecking her lips once more before his phone began to ring.

Before answering, he saw the call was from his brother and tapped Koko's thigh. "I have to make a run really quick." He told her. She knew that it if he was leaving this time of night it must have something to do with his business choice. "I'm going to come back though."

"Okay. I might be sleep so just uh…just take my key." She said shyly.

He smirked and grabbed the set of keys off the coffee table, kissed her lips and left out.

Once the front door was shut and locked, and she could hear Cassim's steps disappear up the hall she began to pace back and forth the small living room. "Fuck!" she huffed, feeling the sting of her tears in her whole face. "Fuck!" she panted, placing her shaky fingers onto her tingling bottom lip where Cassim's lips were connected.

At no point did she think that during her undercover mission as Dakota Summers to catch Cash and Caine that she would have fallen in love with one of them. Now it all made sense. She had been failing miserably getting information that would help build a case against the two drug distributors because they were under her nose the whole time. She had met both Cassim and Akira by mere coincidence when she got hungry one night and built genuine friend ships while away from her family and friends. There was no way that now she would have to reveal to them once she had them in handcuffs that her name was actually Ivyana Atkins.

As if she wasn't overwhelmed enough, Detective Gates' name showed up on her ringing phone took the cake.

"Hello?" She greeted, clearing her throat.

"Officer Atkins. Hey, sorry for calling so late. I just wanted to check in. We only have a month left to come up with something before they pull the plug on this and we have nothing. I know you're doing your best, but I think it's time to add in-"

"No!" She yelled, cutting him off. "No, I don't need anyone else involved I'm so close." She lied. The thought of another officer trying to build a case on the people she had grown to love bothered her. Even though it was what she had initially signed up for. "I just haven't gotten to the twins yet. It's really not easy, Gates." She mumbled, like someone would hear her. Cassim had the key to her place so he could walk in at any moment. Her belly ached at just the thought.

"You're close? Well what do you have? I have to be able to give them something to let them know that we're making progress." He told her.

Ivy knew that she had to give Detective Gates something or someone to get him off of her back and so that she wouldn't risk having to put Cassim in handcuffs. They had already taken down most of corner boys tied to them, only for them to be replaced like it was nothing. There was no way he would be willing to hear of anyone other than the higher ups. "There's this guy who works for them," She began, as her heart raced in the process. Cassim was going to hate her. He had just expressed to her how horrible he felt for getting him involved, but it was either Cash or Riz, and Ivy had to think of Cassim. "His name is Risen. I'm not sure his last name, but he has a lot of blood on his hands." She snitched, feeling her body heat up as each word formed the sentence that would ruin his life. Not only his but all of theirs. Hopefully they wouldn't find anything on him that would stick. Hopefully, what Cassim had said was true. Hopefully he actually could keep him out of trouble. Things were way out of her control now. *"Lord, forgive me."*

TWENTY

. . .

"Well who the fuck is Chyna then Marcus?" Zimora cried and watched Marcus' eyes widen. They had been arguing for an hour with Zimora trying to get her husband to admit he was cheating on her.

"I go to work and come straight home to you, Zim. How the fuck could I be cheating on you?" he had said, causing her to shock his ass his ass with his own secret.

"That's right. I know. I know all about Chyna, and little Mia and Marcus Jr. who'll be here in three weeks." She informed, wiping her unwanted tears from her face.

All of the things that had been thrown, the cruel words that had been said were silenced. There was no sentence he could form to remove the hurt from his wife's face so he said nothing.

"You could've just left." She mumbled. She was tired of yelling and she was tired of trying.

"Why would I leave you? I love you. You know I love you. You're my wife!"

"I'm sure you tell your fiancé the same thing." She chuckled bitterly. "You have a whole family with your mistress! You bought the bitch a ring! I wonder if she knows our nigga isn't shit." She said, pulling her phone from her bosom and finding the contact information she had created for her sister wife.

Zimora knew she couldn't blame Chyna, because she didn't know. She knew that a kid and a half in and an engagement from a married man was enough to make her feel bad enough. But she at least needed to know.

"What the fuck are you doing?" he snapped, like he wasn't just confessing his love only minutes before. He went to snatch the phone out of her hand, but missed it and ended up roughly grabbing her ponytail to pull her back. "Stop playing."

"Damn, you're going real hard about a bitch that's not me!" She reminded, not afraid of his need to be intimidating.

Her father was on the way and she knew Mark wouldn't dare try it in front of the honorable Judge Freeman.

"Call her over. We all might as well get acquainted and shit, right?" she wondered, although she had already hit the call button.

Marcus put both hands on his head and backed into the wall, sighing. His reaction told Zimora that there was nothing he could ever say to make her believed that he loved her ever again.

"Hello?" The girl asked once she picked up. Cars and wind could be heard heavily in the background, making it apparent that she was outdoors.

"Hi, Chyna. You don't know me, but my name is Zimora Pitts. I know this is going to sound crazy, but I'm actually Marcus' wife. I just found out about the two of you." She said, like she was leaving a voicemail to one of her clients. "Actually, the four of you. I was wondering if by any chance you could meet with Marcus and me here at our place?" Marcus stared straight ahead at nothing in particular, listening to the dead silence on Chyna's end.

"Hello?" Zimora asked making sure the call hadn't been disconnected.

"He's there?" She asked, trying to mask her shaky tone.

The noise of her background came back into play, leading Zim and Marcus to believe she had put them on mute to take it all in.

"Yes, he's right here. I'll send you the address." She told her and they both quickly ended the call. "In the meantime, you can go pack your shit up and head back with Chyna when she leaves."

Mark chuckled. "Bitch, this is my house. I'm not going anywhere."

"Bitch, huh?" a husky voice said, announcing his entrance through the cracked door.

Marcus was unpredictable and had put hands on her on many occasions for many different reasons so she wasn't sure how he would react to her knowing about his other life. He had a habit of flipping his wrong doings on Zimora, so she didn't put much past him. Her father was her best friend, so when she called him crying and told him that Marcus had cheated on her he had told her he was hitting the expressway from Jersey.

"Hey daddy." Zimora greeted, trying her best to wipe her tears before he could notice them.

"Is that any way to talk to your wife?" His attention was solely on Marcus, and while Marcus was no bitch, his father in law was six feet even with the law standing behind the ass whooping he was always so close to getting.

Marcus didn't bother responding to the rhetorical question. Instead, they all stood in the kitchen staring at one another. Marcus didn't understand why they needed a chaperone, but his wife was the definition of a daddy's girl and seemed to tell him everything. Too much if he was being honest, but he knew that if he really knew everything his head would be apart from his body already.

"Daddy, could you just take these bags to your car? I can't fit everything into mine."

"What?" Marcus asked, snapping his head to the side to look at his wife. "You're leaving?"

Using that as his cue, Zeus grabbed his daughters' bags and put them in his car. He'd let his daughter and her husband argue as much as they needed to, finding peace in knowing that she wouldn't stand for being treated anything less than she deserved.

"Of course I'm leaving. You just made it clear that you had no intention to, what the fuck else am I supposed to do?"

"Stay! What the fuck!" Mark yelled, paying no mind to the duh expression on her face. "You're my wife!"

"You sure the fuck don't act like it!" She yelled back, feeling her emotions beginning to get the best of her again. "How dare you try to ask me to stay with you after this. Not only did you lie and cheat on me, you built an entire fucking family! What the fuck is wrong with you?"

"Well you didn't want to have my baby!" He growled, and Zimora might have felt bad if he hadn't found out that his first child was born before that had even gotten married. "And you wonder fucking why!" She finished before yet another person had walked through the unlocked door.

Seeing that Marcus was actually there and engaged in a heated argument with the girl from the phone, Chyna knew that the allegations were true. "Hi." She mumbled, directing her attention to Zimora.

"Hi. I'm actually leaving in a little while. I just wanted you to know so we wouldn't go another four years being lied to by this piece of shit. For the sake of your family, he's all yours."

"Man." Marcus said, like he had something to say that would follow it. There was a lot he wanted to say to Chyna. He had already apologized to his wife ten times over, but the guilt he felt for stringing Chyna along the way he did was proving to be a little more painful. He knew he wasn't shit. Zim even knew he wasn't shit. But Chyna thought she had the man of her dreams and he had never seen her eyes so distant or her face holding so much pain. Still though, there was nothing he could say to ease her mind while his wife was right there. And he was sure that he'd never get another opportunity.

"Nigga, shut the fuck up!" Zimora spat just before her father walked back in.

The elephant in the room was of course, Marcus' cheating ass. But as Chyna's hazel eyes bored into Zimora's matching ones, Marcus' cheating took a back burner. Zim's father slowly walked over to where his daughter stood and Chyna looked at him as well. She had never known what her father looked like, but growing up she knew she looked nothing like her mother. So with this man standing before her, sharing the same light skin, jet black hair and hazel eyes as her, she knew that after twenty-nine years…she had found him. *She knew.*

"Do you know me?" She asked lowly, directing her attention to Zeus while Zimora watched. She could've been wrong and her mind could have been playing tricks on her, so she had to ask. And he nodded. She didn't think she looked like her mother, but he could tell that under eye beauty mark

205

anywhere. Her mother had the same one. It seemed to be the only feature that she hadn't gotten from him.

"Did you always know me?" She asked wondering if she really wanted to know the answer.

When he sighed and looked toward Chyna's fiancé's wife, Chyna knew that even if he did know, Zimora didn't.

"I was engaged when I met Celeste. Engaged to Zimora's mother, my now wife, Rocsi. We were young and weren't really sure if we were really going to get married. It all sounded good at the time, but we weren't ready just yet. I wasn't ready. I knew I wasn't, because when I first met Celeste at a pizza store my first thought was how beautiful she was. Before I knew it, I had a girlfriend and a fiancé. I let Celeste fall in love with me knowing that I was preparing to marry the woman of my dreams. Before I could do that though, I had to end things with Celeste. She told me that she had something to discuss with me, so I figured we could both put everything on the table at once. But while I was telling her we could no longer see each other because I was preparing for my wedding, she was telling me that she was six weeks pregnant." He confessed and could feel the steam and embarrassment radiating off of his secret love child. He hated to be meeting her and breaking her all at once, but he had honestly waited almost thirty years to get it off of his chest.

"I won't ever forget the hurt that was on her face and that was never my intention. To hurt her, or anyone." He continued, shifting his attention between his two daughters while Marcus sat uncomfortably on the couch listening to the familiar tale. "I told her I would still be there for her and for the baby, you. She told me okay, but once I left that day I had never seen her again. I got a letter from her about two years later, a little while after Zimora was born. She sent it to my brother's house out of respect for my wife and wrote in the letter how apologetic she was for keeping you away from me, but said that she would feel even worse about our situation if my wife found out that not only did I cheat, but had a child on her. She told me your name and sent me a few pictures, and assured me that I didn't need to worry about either of you. She said that she was dealing with someone else and falling in love and they had been talking about marriage. She told me that he was a great father figure to you and that you would both be okay. I reached out to her on your fifth birthday, because it was killing me that I had a child I wasn't there for, no matter what the situation was. But by then she was married, with twin boys and I felt like maybe she was right and I should step back. So that's what I did." He finished.

Zimora always admired her father's honestly. How no matter the situation, if you asked him something he'd give you the honest truth. Still though, her mind was all over the place. "So you're telling me," She began with a chuckle. "That my husband's fiancé, and the mother of his children just so happen to the sister I never knew I had?" The question was obviously rhetorical and Chyna was glad, because she could already feel the lump in her throat and wouldn't dare let her emotions out in front of three strangers. "Well at least you didn't get the chance to ruin my family the first time. This time doesn't seem so bad." she spat unintentionally, and noticed the disappointment on her father's face instantly. When she invited Chyna over initially, she had no issue with her and actually grateful for her. She had prayed for God to give her a sign that Marcus wasn't the one for her and there it stood, plain as day. But allowing her to have both her husband and her father wasn't a part of her plan.

Chyna had been waiting her entire life to finally find out who had aided her mother in her creation, and even at damn near thirty it brought tears to her eyes. But it wasn't the beautiful moment she was hoping for. His story was touching and she appreciated his honesty. She didn't hate him or her mother now that she understood, but here she was yet again feeling like the reject. First she was reject of her own family, the one child that wasn't of her step father's blood, then she was the reject of her father's family, obviously, and she was even the reject of the family she started with the man she loved.

"Well at least you seem to have a type." She joked, finally directing her attention to Marcus then back toward Zeus and Zimora, through silent tears. "Sorry for following in my mother's footsteps and being the slutty side chick and ruining you guys' family yet again. I really didn't know. Nice meeting you two I wish you all the best." She said quickly as she was headed toward the door, clutching her pregnant belly tightly.

"Chyna," Zeus, her father called while Marcus watched silently and attentively at the hurt that dressed both her and Zimora's faces. She left though before anything after her name could pass his lips.

It was silent in the spacious home and Marcus' frustration was written all over his face. He knew that he had fucked up, and it hurt him to know how badly he had hurt his wife. He hadn't thought the situation all the way through and had found himself in way too deep way too fast. But even still, it was an issue that he had caused. Chyna had no idea about Zimora just like Zimora had no idea about Chyna, or the kids. She was upset, but she had directed her anger to Chyna who was just as hurt, and rightfully so. "You have every right to be upset, but you didn't have to do her like that." He told her.

"You don't have to leave, I'll book a room. Don't worry I won't be at her house. She won't want me either."

With that, Marcus migrated to the back to toss a few necessities into a Nike duffle bag.

"For once, that nigga is right." Her father agreed, making her eyes widen. She hated the thought of disappointing her father or doing anything he might disapprove of. "She really didn't deserve the low blow you hit her with. That was on me. She's pregnant for God's sake. And just found out her father is also the father of the man she thought she was marrying's wife. I'm sure she's been embarrassed enough for a lifetime. All side chicks, or whatever you call them, aren't horrible people. Half the time, they might not even be aware that's what they are."

"Oh like your sidechick?" Zimora spat.

"Watch your fucking mouth." Her father roared and she instantly backed down. Her father was her best friend, but she knew that she had crossed a line and he didn't tolerate disrespect.

"Well what do you want me to do?" Zimora asked feeling defeated. "Let it go?"

"Never. Just remember who you're supposed to be upset with. I thought I taught you better than that." He finished, pecking her forehead. "I'll go get your things and bring them back in. I'll send a locksmith over once he leaves." Zeus said as Marcus was walking out of their shared bedroom.

He stood against the wall of the door and stared at his wife. He saw how even a small glance at him made tears stream from her eyes. But unbeknownst to him, her tears weren't those of sadness. Her and Mark's relationship was horrible and toxic and she had a way out. She could've simply left him and let Chyna keep him, but the hurt side of her had fucked up and blew it. Knowing she didn't have it in her to truly leave, she knew that getting Chyna out of the picture meant she was stuck with him.

TWENTY-ONE

. . .

Trinity was getting good at the whole cooking for your man thing. If she could toot her own horn, she would. She had practically moved into Risen's place, telling her parents that his name was Raven and Raven was her partner for a school project. Knowing how dedicated Trini was to her work, they believed her without hesitation. Their trust in her made her feel bad about breaking it often, even if they weren't aware of it.

But Risen wasn't someone her parents would approve of, and she knew that she had no intentions on ending things with him. She was in love with him and couldn't help but think about forever with him.

The delightful scent of steak, homemade mashed potatoes, steamed broccoli and biscuits filled the air. Risen loved the smell and comfort of having a woman around who made sure he ate well every night, even when she wasn't always the best chef. Riz sat comfortably against the leather couch watching ESPN highlights.

"How was class today, babe?" he asked and she smirked knowing that a commercial had to be on for his interest in her to be peaked for the moment.

"It was okay. I have to turn in this assignment after dinner or I'll forget it's due before midnight." She told him, making a mental reminder for herself.

"You didn't have to cook if you had homework Trini." He borderline scolded.

"Now you know." She chuckled. "You deserve it. I'm so happy you aren't out running the streets any more than you have to."

"I just feel like I need to chill a bit. Especially after talking with my brothers. And I mean, it doesn't hurt that I have you keeping me occupied." He flirted before watching her hesitantly turn the television off. He eyed her like she was crazy forcing her to give him a look letting him know that whatever she wanted to talk about was important.

He followed her to the circle shaped table and his mouth began to water instantly from the aroma and view before him. "Damn, you cooking steak dinners for your man huh?" he joked and she pecked his lips.

"Anything for my man."

"Well what's the occasion? What's so important that you have to tell me over this delicious meal? I mean, I'm not complaining but."

Trini was afraid as time winded down for her to let him know what had been going on. She was afraid of what his reaction would be. She was afraid of what her parents and sister would think. She had stopped praying for a while, but began praying again that they wouldn't look at her like a disgrace because she hadn't only fallen for a bad boy. But got pregnant by him at only twenty-years old with two years of school left. But who could be upset with bliss? Who could be upset about a baby that wasn't a mistake, but one made from love?

The timer on the oven dinged causing Trinity's palms to sweat as she ran over to shut it off and retrieve the contents. She sat the pan of biscuits on the set of towels closest to him and waited for him to catch on that she was trying to let him know about her bun in the oven. She had found the idea on the Internet and knew instantly that she should've chosen another route. His confused expression compelled her to back away and stare at him a little longer.

"Eat baby. You're starting to act a little off."

"I'm pregnant." She blurted out in response before stepping back a little more. She wanted to get a full view of his body language and expressions upon receiving the news. In less than a year, he would be a father.

"Huh?" he asked as he stood, dropping his fork onto his plate. "What you say?"

"Riz," she started as he walked closer to her. "I'm pregnant. Seven weeks according to the stick-" she tried to finish, but he attacked her lips with his own, proving that he actually was excited. She sighed of relief and let out a breath she had no idea she was holding.

"Damn we're creating life together?" He smiled, flashing his braces her way and making her melt.

"We are." She smiled happily. It didn't matter who was or wasn't on board, but at least her man was. It was like a breath of fresh air. But the fresh air got stuck in her chest once she heard loud banging on the door. "Philly PD, open up."

Everything was moving so fast, but seemed to be in slow motion. Neither Trinity or Risen had the chance to move before a boot connected with the wooden door, sending it crashing and falling from the hinges. Riz, as if already familiar with the procedure raised his hands. "Risen Ghould, you are under arrest for the-" they said, but Trini's ears began to ring. She heard nothing. She only saw them taking the father of her unborn child away in handcuffs.

TWENTY-TWO

. . .

Zimora rushed through the doors of the precinct and flashed her badge with a quickness before letting the woman before her know that she was there to see her client, Risen Ghould. She had to quickly throw a pair of slacks over her bare legs and a wrinkled white top. She had already seemed to miss a small chunk of the interrogation once she barged through. "That's enough. Don't say anything else." She demanded, quickly going to stand by her client's side.

Detective Gates smirked at Riz who shot daggers through him before standing with a shrug. "We have all that we need already anyway." He lied and Zim knew it. Hell, anyone knew that if he really had all he needed Riz would be in a cell already. They left out leaving just Risen and Zimora and Zim didn't hesitate to sit beside her client, scooting her chair up and resting her elbows on the table.

"What are they trying to charge you with?"

"Murder one." He said, feeling his heart drop as the words left his lips. "They're trying to say I killed a judge."

"What the fu- What?" Zimora asked with widened eyes. "What did you say? What did you do?" Zim huffed.

Being a criminal defense lawyer was a lot, but to represent the top drug dealers and distributors was even harder. But they paid top dollar, which was well deserved in her mind. It was twice as hard trying to prove their innocence. Especially the higher up on the food chain they got and how badly the city wanted their heads.

"Man, I didn't say shit. They don't have anything on me. If they did I wouldn't be in this damn interrogation room right now. You know that." He was right. And they both knew that if they were able to pick him up from his home, something wasn't right.

"They're going to be looking though. Understand that." Zimora told him. "You better get rid of anything that you need to get rid of." She mumbled, in a warning tone.

Zimora took pride in her integrity even before undergrad and before taking her LSAT for law school. But her goal was to win cases, and sometimes integrity wouldn't guarantee that. Especially if she wanted a guilty man to walk free.

"I've really been chillin' though. Real shit." He huffed, running his hands through his short, soft curls even though his wrists were still in cuffs. "I've been more chill than I've ever been. Something isn't right." He said out loud although they were both thinking it. He looked up at her with pleading eyes. "I'm about to be a dad."

She sat back against her seat and tried to hide the frustration on her face knowing that the officers might still be watching although they weren't able to listen.

"Just relax for tonight. Like you said, they have nothing on you. Just don't say anything and you'll be out of here by the time the sun comes up." She assured, knowing he really needed to hear it. But he knew he was fucked. His fate had been sealed long before that.

Risen wasn't afraid of prison. He had been more than a few times whether it be group homes, juvenile, centers or adult jail and prison. He had been to it all and knew eventually he'd end up back. But now that his life was going well, he had no desire to go back. He had found love for the first time since his grandmother's death and liked that there was something else that could occupy his time. His woman. He was preparing to go to school in only about two months and become a father in less than a year. How could he be going back to jail now? He couldn't have been that fucked up of a person for God to wait until everything was going right for him to be reintroduced to Karma.

Risen's leg shook as his mind raced for the few seconds he was in the room alone after his lawyer had left. Detectives had gone back in, but Detective Gates wasn't among them and Riz knew that he needed to utilize a phone call even if he would be out by the time morning came.

While he was being escorted to a holding cell, Trinity was clutching her phone tightly in her hand. She thought that

221

by the time she released it, it must have water damage from her sweat. She looked around Riz's disoriented home wondering why they even needed to fuck it up during a search when they already claimed to have what they needed to arrest him. Everything was so good literally moments before. Now, here she was looking at the half eaten steak dinner that he couldn't even finish. She was completely overwhelmed. And on top of that, she didn't even turn her assignment in.

But unbeknownst to her, outside in his driveway Detective Gates stood staring at everything from the grass to Risen's parked car. The neighborhood was quiet, with tons of foreign cars so he seemed to blend in with his environment. But Detective Gates knew him and knew he was nothing like the uppity white and boujie black people in his neighborhood. He wasn't supposed to be there, but he had to make sure that if he couldn't get Cash or Caine, he got the next best thing. Officer Atkins had done well with giving him Risen Ghould. He was surprised she had actually gotten to him. He was almost as hard to access as the twins. But the thing he had that the twins didn't was a record. He was perfect. And with him being away, the twins would be running around like chickens with their heads cut off. They'd get their own selves caught up eventually.

But at the moment, they only had what was given to them by their undercover, Officer Atkins and the knowledge Detective Gates already had on the twenty year old. So in order for them to stick him with a case and get him a sentence, he had to do what he had to do. Which was why he was using they keys obtained from Risen's home to pop the trunk to plant the nine millimeter inside, but to his surprise behind an old hoodie and gas can there was a gun of his own. "Well, shit." He mumbled, tucking the gun back at his waist and using a glove to pick up the other, placing it into a clear plastic bag as evidence that was retrieved from the home. If he were lucky, this actually would be a gun tied to a murder.

"Got him."

TWENTY-THREE

...

A loud bang on the door startled a sleeping Dakota as she eyed the green numbers on the clock that sat by her bed. She assumed that her reality had begun to give her bad dreams, but when she realized that the banging hadn't stopped, she shot up out of the bed and ran over to the door. It was after two in the morning, so her gut was telling her that it had to be Cassim.

"Open the door, Dakota." He mumbled, knowing her well enough to know she was standing by the door too afraid to ask who was there.

She opened the door quickly, and Cassim walked through even quicker. "Hey babe. Where are my keys? What's wrong?" she asked all at once as she watched him pace back and forth briefly, deep in thought. For the first time, she was nervous. She found herself wondering if maybe he knew. She was never concerned before because she never knew that her new friends and her new man were who she had been looking for all along.

"Cassim?" she called lowly as she slowly reached her hand out to grab his.

His Ferragamo high tops moved his body toward her, allowing her to wrap her arms around his torso. She could feel forever in his embrace, and dreaded the day when she'd have to hear goodbye in his words. He pulled away and put her keys in her hands.

"I forgot which key went where, but listen. I know I said I would keep you out of all of this," he began. "But I need you."

"What do you need?" She asked eagerly and it was like music to his ears. She never questioned anything he asked of her and that was one of the things he loved about her. She trusted him and knew that in anything that he suggested, she'd be in good hands so she was never worried.

"Go to Kira's house tonight. I want y'all two to just chill there all day. I know you're off tomorrow, but go to work tomorrow night like normal and do a few hours for me. Scope everything out as you work. Let me know if anything

225

suspicious is going on or if there's anyone there who doesn't look like they belong. If there is please text me. Send me pictures if you can. When you can get away, go into the back and through the door that says manager. There's a safe on the floor under the table. 5299 is the code. I need you to clear it. Just throw it all into one of those big ass bags you have and stick it in your trunk. Then go back to Akira's." he told her and they both knew she had a lot of questions and possible objections, but she nodded her head up and down instantly.

They could both feel how fast her heart was beating against her chest. He looked down at her and pecked her lips sweetly. "You scared?" he asked. She looked up at him, swallowing the lump in her throat.

"I'm scared something is going to happen to you." She told him honestly. He couldn't guarantee at that moment that it wouldn't, so he leaned in again and kissed her once more. She accepted his kiss, and parted her lips for him to deepen it. She sniffled, feeling tears beginning to roll down her face. He pulled back and brushed them away. Taking her tears as fear, he wanted to give her some peace of mind.

"They got Riz, tonight." He told her and her body tensed up. She prayed he didn't feel it. "They're trying to pin a body on him, just to get to us and it's fucking with me right now. I'm going to be cool though so don't worry."

Koko nodded, understandingly but absentmindedly crying harder, but her tears were far deeper than that.

"Something doesn't make sense though. I think someone has been watching us so-" he huffed, cutting himself off. "It's getting real hot." He finished looking down at Koko.

"Just leave." She blurted out before she was able to remind herself that this was her job and the case she was risking. But she couldn't look in front of her and think about never seeing him again. "Why don't you and your brother just go? And Akira. Why don't you all just go to Jamaica for a while?" She suggested and he shook his head, making her speak more to sway his decision. "Just for a little while. Until things blow over. I don't want-"

"I'm not a runner. You think I'm going to let everybody who helped me build this shit go down while I'm on an island somewhere? It doesn't work like that. What kind of nigga would I be if-"

"A smart one." Koko said, cutting him off. "Please baby, just go." She was practically begging.

If he didn't leave, then everything was going to hit the fan and either way, she and Cassim would be done.

"Please." She cried, feeling herself begin to panic. Her body began to shake as she cried and hyperventilated. Cassim wrapped his arms around her. He held her tightly for a few seconds before pecking her cheek. *"I can't do that."*

TWENTY-FOUR

• • •

Dakota was a nervous wreck and Akira was trying to keep her calm with her own calm demeanor. She claimed that she was used to cautionary moments and they were nothing to worry about, but it sounded rehearsed. Either way, she was wrong. Koko knew she was wrong because she wasn't going off of feelings. She was going off of information that had already gotten one of their members arrested. And it was information that she herself had leaked. But still, Kira didn't know all of that, but she did know that they had picked Risen up for a murder charge and she seemed way too calm.

"Relax Koko. If you're going to do this, you have to calm down. People can smell fear."

She was right. That was a phrase that was taught at the academy. But Koko tried to calm herself down anyway to match her friends'. But unbeknownst to her, Akira wasn't thinking about the charges. She was thinking about how the police were able to get Riz in the first place. Being around Cairo so long made her adapt the mentality that everyone was a suspect, just like him. She knew that there had to be an informant somewhere and she wouldn't be at peace until she knew who it was.

"You'll be okay though. I'm about to go to the restaurant." Akira mentioned as Dakota was slipping her feet into her floral, chunky heels.

"Where are you going? I thought we were supposed to stay here."

"Girl, you're going to work and I am too. I'll be back when I get off." She snickered before walking toward the door but stopping in her tracks instantly.

Koko adjusted the bun in her head and put on a light coat of lip gloss but the only thing Kira noticed were her shoes. They were very cute, but seemed very familiar.

Your shoes are so cute

Akira's mind flashed backed to a sunny day in March. She remembered the day vividly because it was the day she and

230

Cairo had begun acting on the flirting that had been going on for quite some time. She was having a bad day and decided to opt as delivery driver for the day and had spent the entire day on the phone with Caine.

"Aren't you busy?" she playfully huffed when he wouldn't hang up the phone with her.

"Not too busy for you." He told her, and from then out, she was sold. "Drop your location for me so I can pull up on you real quick." He had suggested and she playfully rolled her eyes but did as she was told since they had a meeting that same night.

She was on a natural high as she made some of her last deliveries. Her bad day had turned into the best and she never wanted to forget anything about that day. Which is probably why she remembered that as she was leaving, a young woman was moving in. Akira could vaguely remember what she wore, but she remembered that the girl had sandy brown hair, a box in hand and those black and floral chunky heels. "*Maybe it was a mere coincidence*" Akira tried to tell herself. And she would've believed it if it weren't for the distinct soft voice she had and her bare, baby face. The way she spoke thank you then and her thank you over the course of their friendship were the same, but she hadn't even realized it. Not until that moment.

Her eyes widened with confused speculation as she quickly grabbed her phone, prepared to call her boyfriend. "I'm about to go." She told Koko and didn't wait for her response before leaving.

The bar was packed and Koko wondered if she would even be able to notice suspicion on a crowded Friday night, but she was looking. In her mind, she owed Cassim. Growing up, she had always wanted to be a detective. If being a patrol officer first weren't a requirement, she wouldn't even be in the situation she was. She knew that by being on such a big case, she would be able to get higher up quicker. But growing up, she always wanted to be a wife and mother as well. And when she was with Cassim, she imagined how dapper he'd look on their wedding day and what their future children might look like. He made her feel like a high school student again. The way she felt about men before reality set in that they weren't shit. He made her believe in love again. And if he found out that not only was she an officer, but responsible for Risen's arrest by using pillow talk information he would hate her.

Her phone rang just before her shift began and when she read 'dad' her heart fell. She hadn't spoken to her father, mother, or her sister in a week and she missed them. She made a note to call her real father as she picked up the decoy call for Detective Gates.

"Ivy, you did so great I could kiss you!" He yelled, forcing her to turn the volume down although she was alone. "We found a gun in Risen Ghould's apartment. We sent it to ballistics and would you believe it, it's the same gun that killed Judge Banks? That on top of his saliva found near the crime scene," he clapped. "We got this son of a bitch." He said and Koko stood emotionlessly. *This is the part where I jump for joy, huh?* "We can offer him a deal where if he could give up the twins he'd face no charges. He'll have no choice but to turn over Cash and Caine or he'll be facing life for sure. It's incredible!" he said and her heart began to race.

That wasn't what she had in mind at all. She was sure Risen would be enough, now she had sacrificed him and they were still going after the twins. "Are you ready to take your mask off Ms. Atkins? We're going to pick him up tonight and I want you to do the honors,"

Seeing that there was no suspicious going on inside of the bar, probably because her colleagues felt like they had enough to convict, she migrated to the back like she was told. She listened to her superior speak as she unlocked the safe and emptied its contents inside of her large bag. She was almost nervous that all of the money wouldn't fit, but she was able to fill the entire bag with cash and two guns before zipping it up. She quickly walked out, with her phone to her ear and placed the bag in the trunk before releasing a breath and responding.

"You want me to do it? No, Jonathan, I-"

"I insist. I'm proud of you." He said.

"Oh- Okay. Yeah." She said as she looked down at an incoming call from Cash. "Give me an hour at least. I'm at work." She chuckled nervously.

"Dedication. I love it. Nine o'clock at his place." She looked at the time on her car radio seeing that it was eight pm exactly before answering her boyfriend's call just before the ringing stopped.

"Hey baby." Koko greeted. There was noise in his background that was silenced before he spoke. "Hey beautiful. You good?"

"I'm good. I'm in the car now on my way back to Kira's" She told him, letting him know that he had done what he asked.

"Thank you. I'm glad I can trust you." His words were genuine on his end, but she couldn't help feeling like he was reading through her deceit. "We're all about to meet up at Riz's place to try to figure out how to keep his ass low and out of jail. Just meet us there. I want you with me." He admitted and Koko was sure her anxiety was going to get the best of her.

"Do you think that's smart, babe?" I mean the police just kicked his door down a day ago and that's where you guys want to meet?"

"I'm good." He responded simply letting her know that it wasn't up for debate.

"No, Cassim listen."

"I'm good, Dakota. I love you." He told her.

His words forced tears to trickle down her cheeks. She knew that he had slipped up before, but he had never opened his mouth and let "I love you" fall out alone. But she believed him. Because if he felt about her the way she felt about him, there was no other way to explain the feeling. "I love you more."

She could hear him smiling through the phone and it made her heart flutter.

"Akira keeps blowing my phone up. Let me see what she wants and I'll see you when you get there." He said and waited for her to say bye before he switched calls.

As she put the car in drive, she had no idea where the fuck she was supposed to go. Detective Gates was awaiting Ivy's arrival at Risen's home to arrest him, while Cassim was waiting on Koko to arrive at the same location. "Maybe I'll just drive off a cliff." She whined, in defeat. There was no way for her to get out of this. But since she was due at Risen's house earlier than Detective Gates would be there, maybe she could get them out before he got there. She nodded at herself in approval and pulled off.

But as she made it to the first stoplight her mind began to race. When the case first began, Detective Gates said the only bit of information they had was that the boys were twins. Yet, Cash had told her nobody knew they were twins unless they were close enough to. Like his family and the people he worked with. And since Jonathan was so adamant on getting them, she was beginning to wonder if in fact he did know them beyond the case.

TWENTY-FIVE

. . .

Trinity walked around the house eating a bowl of grits even though it was after eight at night. She was only a little under two months pregnant and not showing at all, but the cravings and food aversions made sure to remind her that she was indeed carrying a child. She picked up a piece of glass that she had seemed to miss after the police had fucked up Risen's house.

The front door creaked and made her nervous instantly. She ran to the door, almost teary eyed. Riz getting arrested had fucked her up and she was afraid for him to ever be out of her sight.

"Where are you going?" She wondered, grabbing ahold of his wrist protectively.

"I was just looking outside." He told her. He looked at the time on his watch and furrowed his brows. Cash and Caine were supposed to be there already. He was paranoid himself.

He knew that he needed to get them into a new home and quick for the both of their sakes. You can't put a price on peace of mind. "I told you that Cash, Caine, Kira and Cash's girl are on their way so we can figure out what the fuck we need to do." He told her, huffing before shutting the door. She stared at him. The straining features in his face saddened her. "I'm just real stressed right now, babe. I am." He admitted. "I'm not feeling right. Something doesn't feel right."

She wrapped her arms around his torso to comfort him, but the cologne he wore that she loved had her stomach doing flips and her mouth moistening with saliva. She gagged slightly, placing an opened hand over her mouth and ran to the bathroom. She left Riz in the living room along with the harsh reality that he was going to jail and wouldn't get to see his child being born. He knew that he had done a lot of shit and soon it would all catch up with him. Now was his time. He always knew it would come, but he never expected to be in the place he was currently when it did. He was in love, about to go to college and had even begun making plans for his twenty-first birthday already. He had a kid on the way. A chance at giving his child the father he never had. How could he do that from prison? Being with Trinity showed him all of the things that he actually could do. They had exposed one another to so much. He had gotten her streets smarts levels up while she reminded him of all the things he couldn't remember from school. She helped him get his GED and had helped him enroll in college courses at her school.

Hearing her small, quick feet make their way back over to him Risen sat up and wiped his hand down his face. She noticed the expression on his face anyway and could feel his defeat.

"I'm going to jail, baby." He told her and she began to cry instantly. "Nah, don't do that." He begged. "I've done way too much to try to cheat fate. It's inevitable for me."

"You can't. Let's just leave. Where should we go? I'll go get our tickets!" She panicked, grabbing her laptop from the end table closest to her. Trinity was in love and couldn't see herself without him. Especially now that she was carrying their child.

"Trini, it's too late for that. I can't leave the state while they're investigating. One sight of my ID and they'll be right on my ass."

Trinity's tears wouldn't let up as she began to take everything in. "Well what can we do then? Will they come here again? How does this work? When are – what?" she said, jumbling her words together in a nervous wreck.

"Just relax. Chill." He told her as well as himself.

"How the fuck do you expect me to chill?" She snapped. "To fucking relax? Do I look like I can fucking relax? You're in my face telling me, your girl, the mother of your unborn that you won't be around and I'm supposed to chill?"

"You don't have a fucking choice!" He yelled back.

"My sister is a cop. Maybe she can help." She said as she picked up her phone to call Ivy only for it to ring until the voicemail picked up.

"I'm sure this is beyond her control, babe." He told her, lowering his tone. She was making things way harder for him. "I have a record. A charge on top of that, a murder charge on a judge at that, that's a death sentence." He told her, facing his own reality.

Risen chuckled to himself before shaking his head and biting his lip realizing that all of his crucial years would be spent in jail. He was only twenty and preparing to face a life sentence in prison.

"What if I take it?" she suggested, remembering that it seemed to be the ultimate hood test of loyalty. "What if I just say I did it? They have a gun with no fingerprints I can easily say it was mine. They have a case. You just don't necessarily have to be the one who goes down for it."

"Fuck no! Are you out of your fucking mind yo? Who do you think you're talking to?" He asked, growing angry that she would ever fix her lips to say such a thing to him. She was pregnant, pregnant with his child. There was no way she was going to jail. And what kind of nigga would he be if he let her?

"Just hear me out. Listen," She said as she placed her fingertips on her temples and paced back and forth. "I don't have a record at all. My parents are super religious devout Christians and my sister is a cop. There's no way they'd give me that much time, right?"

"Wrong! This is a judge, Trinity! They don't care who you are, you're doing some time behind that."

Young, naïve Trinity didn't believe that. She wouldn't accept that. Her sister wouldn't ever let that happen. Cops were above the law, clearly. So she knew her sister would be able to make sure she didn't rot in a cell when they didn't have all evidence point to anyone anyway. She shook her head from side to side. "I've seen some of my friends' parents say that their father's killed people in their day and they were home to spend all of their crucial years with them. We can do this. We can beat this and be a family." She nodded through tears. Her decision was made.

"Their fathers were probably snitches." He spat. "Fuck no. You're not doing that. I have a good lawyer. She's going to fight for me and what happens from there is that happens." He told her putting his foot down.

"Just stay out of trouble, please?" She begged. "So when I do get home we won't ever have to be in a situation like this again. My record won't be clean anymore so we won't be able to afford it."

Risen stared at her growing furious. She wasn't listening to him and he wasn't trying to hear shit that she was talking about. He would never let her do that, so he wasn't sure why she was talking to him like the decision was final.

"Listen, go home okay babe?" He said softly. If he made her believe that he was down for it, she would just leave it alone. "Take a bath at your parents' house and relax where you can have some peace of mind. I'll come over tomorrow and we'll figure everything out. Okay?" He asked and she nodded. He sighed, grateful that she hadn't put up a fight.

"Okay. Let me call my sister again though. I really just want to know if there's anything that can be done. Or I won't sleep tonight." She admitted while grabbing her bag from the couch and placing her computer inside.

With her phone tucked between her shoulder and ear, she packed up her things and listened to it ring. She and Riz continued to talk, while she listened to the phone ring on her end until it could be heard outside of the door. The confused expression on her face didn't even last long before she was hit with Déjà vu. She looked toward the door, then the phone in her hand and back before the new door was kicked in and fell off the hinges yet again.

Four officers barged in, Ivy Atkins being one of them.

"Risen Ghould," she began as she pulled cuffs from her side. "You're under arrest for the murder of Judge Julian Banks." She told him in a stern, rehearsed tone and both he and Trinity's eyes widened. Risen could feel that she was going to go against the grain and do the exact thing he told her not to do. He shook his head at her discreetly, but even still her mind was made up. Her unborn needed both of their parents. She wasn't letting her man go to jail for life.

"Trini." He forewarned while burning a hole into her that she pretended not to see.

"He didn't do it. I did!" She told them, praying that the lie was believable. Her voice along with her face was stern and she was content in her decisions. She could do a few months in jail. She was sure that's all she would get.

"Trinity?" Ivy yelled, her eyes welling with tears as she finally noticed her baby sister. Trinity's eyes were welled with tears as well, and while Ivy's came from a place of regret, Trinity's came from a place of betrayal.

TWENTY-SIX

· · ·

Caine listened to his brother talk to his girlfriend on the phone and smirked at how he interacted with her as they drove to Risen's house. He couldn't deny that his brother was in love and he was actually happy for him even with all of the shit he had given him. He knew how he felt about Akira and knew that his brother deserved that feeling as well. He drove through the busy, Philly traffic with the radio off so that Cash could hear his conversation, but the silence had him thinking too hard about too much.

Hearing Cash tell Koko that his woman was blowing his phone up made him nervous and he pulled his phone from the cup holder instantly. He was never nervous, which was why he was battling with himself daily about why he was even in a relationship. She brought all of the feelings out of him that he liked to pretend he didn't have. To his surprise, his phone began to ring as soon as he picked it up and as expected it was

Akira. He could feel the urgency in the vibrations before he picked up.

"Hello."

"Are you with Cash?" She asked frantically. She let out a breath of relief when he said yes. She had been calling him back to back trying to voice her theory to him before it was too late.

"Yeah, what's going on?"

"Put the phone on speaker." She demanded and he did, curious about the conversation that was sure to follow.

"Yerp," Cash said, letting Kira know that he heard her, but she immediately began rambling.

"Cash, I know you and Koko have been cozy but I really think she's hiding something. I remember meeting her way before we met her at the restaurant. She was just moving into her apartment building and I was delivering food that day. She had light brown hair and it's just fucking with me a little." She admitted. "She told us that she wasn't new to the neighborhood and everything started going left when she magically appeared and I'm just nervous I can't even lie. That's my bitch. I fuck with her for real, but we have to admit that things started happening right after she arrived." She bellowed out before sighing. She had used all of her breath to get it out and now as she waited in silence with her brother and man, her heart was racing.

Cash and Caine looked at one another briefly.

"I just don't want us to go over Riz's house and it be a set up, you know? I'm not trying to point fingers or make accusations but I'm not stupid either and my gut is really telling me that something is off with her. Cash I'm sor-"

Cassim didn't even really need to hear anymore. He was in love, but he wasn't stupid. That wasn't what heightened his realization though. It was the simple fact that he knew she had to be too good to be true.

"It's cool. You're right." he told her, earning and confused gaze from Caine.

"I am?" She asked and he nodded like she could see.

"Might explain why she was trying to get me to not go to Riz's." He chuckled bitterly, nodding his head up and down.

"She told you not to go?" Caine asked, his voice angry and strong. He placed his foot on the brake, even though it was a green light and earned horns honking behind him. Once Cash confirmed, Caine bussed a U-turn and headed back to the only house that Koko wasn't aware of. Caine's.

"Meet us at the house, Kira." Caine said seeing that his brother didn't have much else to say.

The ride to Cairo's was silent. Even outside of the car seemed to be silent as the traffic appeared to subside but Cash knew it was only a matter of time before Caine gave him his unwanted opinion.

"Wait," Cash said out loud showcasing how deep in thought he was. "If going over to Riz's place wasn't a good idea, why the fuck didn't we just go get him, man." He huffed, rubbing a hand over his face. Stress for him was and understatement.

"What the fuck were we supposed to do? Call him and say hey, meet us at my place so that you can get followed and we all get locked the fuck up?" Caine asked, not caring how it made him sound.

They had put Riz under their wing and looked at him as a younger brother, but he put himself in that situation by being careless. Something they had told him over and over about. He couldn't allow himself to feel bad for him. Those emotions weren't allowed in the game they played. Cash tried to call Risen anyway, to try to tell him why they weren't coming at least, but his phone only rang and rang and rang.

Akira was already parking in one of the two door garages once the boys pulled up. Neither of them spoke until they were all in the house and seated about the large, unnecessary dining room table. They listened to Risen's phone ring over and over again before Akira sighed and finally gave up. They all knew that him not answering the phone couldn't be good. He was supposed to be accessible always for them.

They were sure that they would be getting a call about his arrest at any moment.

While they were all fairly quiet. Cash seemed out of it. His eyes were trained on the wall in front of him like there was no one else around. Truthfully, he wished that there wasn't. He would much rather face his stupidity and embarrassment alone.

"It may not have been her." Kira voiced, not being able to stomach seeing Cassim beat himself up mentally and in pain.

"Shut up. Please. Just-" he continued as he placed his elbows on his knees and his hands under his chin.

"What else could she be?" Caine asked and his voice instantly annoyed Cash. "Once she came around all of our shit came crumbling down. Can't nobody but a cop do shit like that." He told him, using all of his energy to make the 'but' in the sentence pop out. He wanted them to feel it and understand. "And you-" he continued, pointing to his brother. "I told you about that bitch from the fucking rip! She had your nose wide opened and you started pillow talking like a sucker."

"Cai-" Akira warned, hating to see the two brothers fighting. Especially when Cash was already feeling bad enough.

"Fuck you, pussy." Cash spat, not having much else to say since his brother was right.

Cash couldn't get all of the conversations he and Dakota had out of his head or all of the things he had shared with her. He imagined her smile and laughter and wondered how she could fake such intimate moments. How could she have him feeling the best he had ever felt and still stab him in the back? *And the academy award goes to.*

Cash stood, making his way to the kitchen for a small second of loneliness but stopped abruptly when a heavy knock sounded in the living room and echoed throughout the quiet, spacious home. Caine quickly stood, pulling a nine-millimeter handgun from his waist. "Put that shit away, stupid!" Akira yelled, but he paid her no mind.

"Hell no. If they're coming to my house for war, they're going to get it." He swung the door opened without asking who it was and was surprised when he came face to face with Riz.

Quickly, Cairo let him in and looked both ways to make sure he wasn't followed before shutting and locking the door behind them. Risen was out of breath and sweating like he had run all the way to Caine's from his own home that was fifteen minutes away by car. Akira ran over to him and hugged him tightly while Caine and Cash stood side by side waiting for him to get to talking.

"That bitch from the club is a cop!" He wheezed out and they all nodded knowingly which surprised him. He wasn't expecting for their reactions to be so calm. Especially Cash. "They kicked my door in and tried to get me with the murder of the judge I popped in like April. They found the gun."

"How the fuck did they find a gun you got rid of Risen?" Cash snapped. "I told you to get rid of that shit."

"I did!" he yelled. "I swear I did. I know I did." He continued. "I mean, I thought I did. I remember I was driving to the river to dump it. I was on the phone with one of you. Remember? I had wiped it off and everything," he said before pausing. "Fuck."

As he began to replay the day in his head, he remembered bumping into Trinity and her feeling the steel in front of her. "I met my girl that day when I was on my way. I stopped for a second to talk to her and I tossed it in the trunk because I didn't want her to see it." He said out loud, letting his eyes shift from Cash to Caine wondering if they felt like he was as stupid as he felt he was.

"I wasn't thinking. I was distracted and I fucked up." He said, making Cash clench his jaw in understanding. Risen sounded like he was almost ready to cry though, letting them know that there was something else on his mind. And there was. His girl.

"She said she did it. She's trying to take the bid for me but that's a judge, my nigga. That's at least twenty years, record or not record. She thought that her sister was going to be able to get her out but her sister is the one who came to arrest me! The bitch from the club!" He told them, giving them information that they didn't have.

Cash had other questions about Koko, but that moment wasn't the time. Actually, there would never be a time. He prayed he never had to see her again.

"She's pregnant, man. She was trying to make sure I was around for my kid, but now she probably won't be around." He said as he stepped back into the wall to catch his breath.

"Riz, calm down baby. Everything-"

"She's going to have my baby in prison and they're going to snatch it right from her arms." He admitted, cutting Akira off. His eyes glossed over with fresh tears that neither of them was used to seeing. "Do you think they'll give the baby to me? Can they do that or will my baby be in the system like me?"

His cracking voice broke the three of them and Cash shook his head wondering how everything had gone so bad so fast.

He found it admirable how his girl was willing to do something so stupid for him. Idiotic for sure but nothing said love like stupidity. Cash tapped his pocket slightly and left out of the house against the three others' request, but he needed some air and time to comprehend. Plus, he had some business to handle.

Peeling off in one of his brother's cars, he ignored his constant ringing cell phone, knowing it couldn't be anyone but Caine or Kira. He didn't want to talk though. He only wanted to be alone and enjoy the silence as his mind wandered. But looking down at his lit phone, he saw that it was his mother who had called him seven times back to back. His eyes widened as he pulled over, parking in front of a two-story row home. He dialed his mother's number and she answered instantly, speaking in a way he couldn't understand.

She was crying and Cash could feel his chest beginning to rise and fall rapidly. "Mom what's wrong? What happened? I can't-"

"Chyna," was the only word that passed her lips he could make out.

"Chyna? What's wrong, ma?"

"She," she sighed before his father's voice could be heard on the other side as he had taken the phone.

"Cassim,"

"What's going on, pop?" He wondered, finding himself hyperventilating. He could feel that something wasn't right. "Your sister was in an accident. Her car was t-boned and spun, making her crash into a tree. They got her out in time, and said that her stress levels were high and they needed to do an emergency C-section-"

"So she's okay?" Cash sighed, "good. What hospital is she in?" he asked shifting the gear back to drive to head in the direction his father gave him but Legend was silent.
"She died during delivery. Your nephew is fine though. We-" he continued, but Cash didn't hear anything after *she died.*

He wouldn't cry for anything that he was going through, but for his only sister, he banged his head and fists on

258

the steering wheel shedding what seemed like all of the tears he possessed, grateful that he had pulled over. If not, he was sure he wouldn't be able to see the road in front of him. And unbeknownst to him, that was the exact reason his sister was no longer with them.

TWENTY–SEVEN

. . .

Ivy ran into the precinct, bypassing the row of desks and ringing phones and headed straight to the back.

"Nice work Atkins."

"Good job Ivy!" her colleagues congratulated her, but that was the last thing on her mind. These were people who didn't even know of her existence before this case. And she hated everything about what she had to do and especially that her sister got caught in the crossfire. She walked through the blue double doors and down the eight steps to the damp basement where holding was. It wasn't a place that Ivy was very familiar with, but it was the first place she headed to the second she was able.

"I'm looking for my sister. Trinity Atkins. Is she here?" She questioned anxiously and breathlessly as she took another look around.

The petite black woman looked up at her, chewing on a piece of gum that came from the lollipop she had just finished. "She's getting processed right now, give me a-"

"No listen. I don't think you understand. There's been a mistake. She didn't do anything. I need to talk to her.

"Listen sugar, I get it." She cooed like Ivy was a student of hers rather than someone probably above her pay grade. "But evidence in this case was scarce. We have a confession and connection to the initial suspect. We have to run with it."

Ivy tossed her head back as she tried to think and pace her breathing simultaneously.

"Fuck." She mumbled under her breath before the hair on the arms stood and his fragrance tickled her nostrils.

She turned swiftly with wide eyes and met his cold, red ones. She almost mistook him for Cairo by how he looked at her with disgust.

"I was wondering how I could go about posting bail for Trinity Atkins." Cash told the person at the desk. The small woman had been replaced with a bald, older white guy.

"Bail?" He asked with a chuckle. "This woman killed a judge. What bail? She isn't going anywhere" he finished with a shrug. He couldn't care less either way.

Ivy's heart dropped and she couldn't hide the tears that had fallen from her eyes. She had to fix this. Cash had only found out that the pregnant twenty-year old could've potentially been his sister in-law, but he felt for Koko. Especially since finding out that his own sister would no longer be attending their weekly family dinners and getting on his nerves. He knew that the majority of Koko's concern was knowing that her sister was behind bars behind her, but as he looked Koko up and down and noticed her still wearing the bodysuit from Chinx with her badge over top of it, he grew repulsive. He shot another disgusted, lip turned up look to Ivy and shook his head before walking out, crushing her heart in the process.

EPILOGUE

. . .

Three Months Later

Trinity Atkins had never thought that she would get used to being in prison, but she was maintaining pretty well with no trouble at all. Inmates, guards and staff were all unusually cool and she knew that someone had to be looking out for her. And she was almost certain that that someone was her sister, Ivy.

Trinity and Ivy had an amazing bond at one point, but Ivy was the last person Trinity wanted to speak to. She was responsible for everything. She was responsible for the charge against Riz and ultimately the life sentence that she herself was serving. She was responsible for the fact that she hadn't felt loved or beautiful in the past few months.

She grabbed the black handle of the pay phone and put it to her ear before dialing the only number she had been

263

calling since she'd been there. The same number that she still couldn't get through to because it went to voicemail every time. This time though, the phone rang once and Trini rubbed her belly with anticipation. For half a second, her chest tightened and palms began to sweat. She couldn't wait to hear his voice, but after that first ring, an automated service let her know "the number you are trying to reach has been disconnected. Please try again later. Thank you. Goodbye" Click.

Tears trickled down her face as hope flooded out of her by way of her morning sickness. She vomited up everything from breakfast, lunch, and the realization that Risen had left her hanging.

——————————————

A Message From The Author

Thank You!

If this isn't the first book you've read by me, I appreciate your constant love and support. If it is the first book that you've read by me, I hope it won't be the last. I hope you enjoyed.

Love & Blessing,

Miss. Parker

Facebook: Parker Washington

Facebook Like Page: Author Parker Washington

Instagram: ___.danni

C O M I N G S O O N !

CUFFED: A Cautionary Tale of Love, Lies & Betrayal 2

As a thank you for reading, check out this sneak peek!

• • •

Three Months Earlier

Dakota Summers jogged out of the building once the realization that there was nothing she could do for her sister hit her like a ton of bricks. Her skin crawled and her ears rang as her vision blurred from welling tears. As if her heart wasn't already halfway broken, seeing Cassim casually walk back to a truck she had never seen crushed her even more. Her chest ached seeing that she was so far behind and he was growing farther and farther away from her. Her legs were no match for his long ones and though she was finding it hard to keep up, she made it to the passenger side just in time to hop in before he was able to lock the doors.

"Baby," she began, but didn't even have the chance to follow it before his deep voice roared through the confined space.

"Get out," he demanded, not even bothering to waste a gaze on her.

"Cassim, just-"

"Get the fuck out of my car! Officer" he continued, roughly grabbing the badge that hung from her neck, before dropping it like it was hot or was too repulsive for his touch.

His disgusted gaze made her feel small under it and forced a stream of tears from her eyes, but still she couldn't leave. "I didn't know. I swear I didn't." She admitted, not bothering to hide her ugly crying face. She needed him to see sincerity in her eyes. "I'm sorry. I'm so sorry. I promise I didn't know you were my target."

Cassim shook his head and shifted in his seat wondering himself why he hadn't just pushed her ass out. He had no desire to hear an explanation from her, but needed to. Koko removed her badge along with the navy blue jacket with PPD boldly written across her back.

"It's my job. I had to do it. I didn't know it was you though, baby I swear. I didn't know you had a twin and that you two

were who I was supposed to be going after. When I found out
didn't I warn you? Didn't I try to get you to run?" she asked
through tears, trying to make out her words as clear as she
could. She needed him to understand that she didn't possess
vindictive intent.

"You tried to warn me but you didn't tell me!" he snapped,
banging his fist on the steering wheel and accidentally beeping
the horn. "What if I would've been there like I was planning?"
he asked rhetorically. "Oops. I tried to tell you now I'm under
arrest for the rest of my fucking life!"

"Was I supposed to say I'm a cop working a case against you
and your brother but I didn't know so I need you to lay low
while I figure shit out?"

"That's exactly what the fuck you should've said!" he snapped
again causing her to cry harder, holding onto her chest as she
hyperventilated. She hadn't thought about the fact that she
could just be honest with him. She found herself wondering
how things would have turned out if she would have.

For the first time, she was feeling like every aspect of her world was crumbling around her. Cassim was supposed to be the sweet escape, but even he couldn't hide the hurt and disgusted look on his face. "I'm sorry," was the only thing she could think of to say. Taking a chance, she climbed over the middle console and sat in his lap, forcing his eye contact. She grabbed ahold of his chin and saw all of the hurt in his eyes. "I'm so sorry. I love you." She assured rubbing her hands down his face and turned his face back once he looked away.

He wanted to push her off and tell her once again to get out, but her touch was exactly what he needed. He felt complete with her around. He was clearly in love and almost felt like he was betraying himself, his brother and his business because of it.

"I should have told you as soon as I found out. I should have known that I could and I'm so sorry. But I can't lose you. You know I love you," she sobbed, pressing her forehead against his. "Please don't hate me."

While Cassim was pissed beyond words with Dakota, or whatever her real name was, he couldn't pretend like it wasn't the woman he had grown to love. He was vulnerable and needed her, as he still had yet to process his sister's death. He was overwhelmed and that was the only reason he hadn't took it upon himself to personally remove her from his brother's car and never see her again.

Cash leaned his head into his left arm that rested on the door to avoid seeing her cry. Koko grabbed ahold of his chin and slightly pulled his head back before crashing her lips into his. He could feel the wetness from her teardrops on his own face and for a second he thought that maybe if he let a few of his own fall, she wouldn't notice they were his.

"What can I do to make you forgive me? I can see it in your face that you don't. I'm afraid that once I get out of this car I won't ever see you again." She softly murmured.

"What are you willing to do to earn my forgiveness?" he asked finding himself draping his arm around her waist to better position her.

The simple gesture made her melt into his arms and bury her face into his neck while he bit his lip in thought. Cash's battled with his heart and his mind were beginning to bother him. Especially since his heart was winning. He felt stupid for even being in her presence knowing that she was responsible for the havoc of his life recently. But when he thought about it further, he saw that everything seemed to backfire on her. While her intention was to arrest Risen, it was her sister who took the fall. And thinking of her sister made him think of his own. He couldn't imagine how it would feel to have a sister hate him or be behind bars because of him, but he did know how it felt to have his sister gone and it was the most indescribable pain he had ever encountered. While she deserved to know how she hurt him, he'd never want her to hurt that badly. They were in a game of losers.

Moments of comfortable silence passed and Cash realized that she couldn't come up with an answer, he decided for her.

"You love me?" he asked for assurance and felt her nod against him. He tightened his grip around her to make sure she didn't leave once the words etched in his brain traveled passed his lips as words.

"You know I love you, Cassim"

Most of him did know. Shit, all of him knew. He could tell by how she clung to him with her body shaking as she tried to control her breathing. And because he knew, he almost felt bad for thinking what he was thinking. But he had to remind himself that he was a man of business at the end of the day. And since she had brought heat to him, she would have to be the one to fix it.

"Come work for me."

———